This special signed edition is limited
to 1500 numbered copies
and 26 lettered copies.

This is copy __476__ .

SCREAMING
SCIENCE FICTION
HORRORS FROM OUT OF SPACE

Contents

SCREAMING
SCIENCE FICTION
HORRORS FROM OUT OF SPACE

BRIAN LUMLEY

SUBTERRANEAN PRESS 2006

"Snarker's Son," © 1980, *New Tales of Terror*, Ed. Hugh Lamb, Magnum, Methuen, (UK).

"The Man Who Felt Pain," © 1989, *Fantasy Tales*, Vol. 10, No. 2.

"The Strange Years," © 1982, *Fantasy Tales*, Vol. 5, No. 9.

"No Way Home," © 1975, *F&SF*, Vol. 49, No. 3, Mercury Press.

"The Man Who Saw No Spiders" © 1979, *Weirdbook 13*, ed. W. Paul Ganley.

"Deja Viewer," © 2004, *Maelstrom*, Vol. 1, Calvin House.

"Feasibility Study," © 2006, appears here for the first time.

"Gaddy's Gloves," © 1991, "World Fantasy Convention Book."

"Big 'C,'" © 1990, *Lovecraft's Legacy*, ed. Weinberg and Greenberg, TOR Books, USA.

First Edition

ISBN
1-59606-042-5

Subterranean Press
PO Box 190106
Burton, MI 48519
www.subterraneanpress.com
subpress@earthlink.net

Foreword

I HAVE BEEN ASKED on several occasions why I cross genres. In fact on one occasion I was asked why I "stagger" between them. (Oh you, you! I remember you and know where you live!) But you know, that's how it was when I was coming up. I was seeing the movies, reading the comics, and I was into the pulp magazines; so that even before I knew what a "genre" was, it seemed to me that everyone was crossing them. Take a gander at those old EC Comics, you'll soon see what I'm getting at. *The Haunt of Fear* and *Tales from the Crypt* were "horror" horror, but a good many of the tales in *Weird Fantasy* were "fantasy" horror, and many of those in *Weird Science* were horror "SF."

Even H. P. Lovecraft—the Old Gent of Providence himself, known primarily for his superb horror stories—had mixed his genres: *The Shadow Out of Time* and *At the Mountains of Madness* in *Astounding Science Fiction*, for example. (Hey, and HPL took a kicking for it, too!) And then there was Ray Bradbury's wonderful *Martian Chronicles*: whimsical, yes, and written as only Bradbury can write them, but the horror undertones were there. In fact those stories were quite literally *literary* miscegenation, hybrids of all three species of our favorite fictions: Horror, Fantasy, and SF. And, I might add, classics at that.

But if you'll step back from the printed page for a moment and take a look at the big screen, you'll perhaps see far more clearly what I'm getting at. *Predator* was SF/Horror—in fact you could as easily and probably more properly call it Horror/SF! And the same goes for the *Alien* movies—with knobs on—and likewise the *Terminator* films, and *The Fly*, and *The Thing*, etc, etc, ad infinitum. And weren't they all blockbusters, and didn't we enjoy them? Well I did, that's for sure.

And so—with the exception of supernatural horror and so-called splatterpunk, where the science in the horror is mainly absent—it appears to my mind that a large percentage of speculative and fantastic fiction benefits hugely from this miscegenation, the incorporation of horror motifs, and I'm not at all unhappy to admit that most of my weird fiction has at least an element of SF in it, and often a lot more than just an element. "Hard Science Fiction" it most certainly isn't; "weird science" it may well be—but so what? I've always believed that it's my job to entertain, not to edify, though I would like to believe that every so often along the way I may even have been "guilty" of a little of that, too.

Anyway, here it is: a sampler of my Screaming Science Fiction from across the years, a large handful of my Horrors Out of Space. Because hey, if it was good enough for HPL, Ray Bradbury and EC Comics—and since it has *remained* good enough for generation after generation of marvelous Tinseltown movie-makers—it's certainly good enough for me....

Brian Lumley, Devon, UK
January 2005

Snarker's Son

This one harks back to my early days. Written in 1970, when I still had another ten years to go finishing off my Army career, it was scheduled to appear variously in this, that or the other professional and semipro magazine or anthology that all folded, which used to happen somewhat frequently in those days. Finally editor Hugh Lamb bought it for his *New Tales of Terror* anthology, Magnum Books, 1980. A parallel universe story, it's about a small boy who… but no, you really don't want to go there. In case you do, however, I suggest you read on….

"ALL RIGHT, ALL RIGHT!" Sergeant Scott noisily submitted. "So you're lost. You're staying with your dad here in the city at a hotel—you went sightseeing and you got separated—I accept all that. But look, son, we've had lost kids in here before, often, and they didn't try on all this silly stuff about names and spellings and all!"

Sergeant Scott had known—had been instinctively "aware" all day—that this was going to be one of *those* shifts. Right up until ten minutes ago his intuition had seemed for once to have let him down. But now….

"It's true," the pallid, red-eyed nine-year-old insisted, hysteria in his voice. "It's all true, everything I've said. This town *looks* like Mondon—but it's not! And…and before I came in here I passed a store called Woolworths—but it should have been 'Wolwords'!"

"All right, let's not start that again." The policeman put up quieting hands. "Now: you say you came down with your father from…from Sunderpool? That's in England?"

"No, I've *told* you," the kid started to cry again. "It's 'Eenland'!" We came down on holiday from Sunderpool by longcar, and—"

"Longcar?" Sergeant Scott cut in, frowning. "Is that some place on the north-east coast?"

"No, it's not a place! A longcar is…well, a *longcar*! Like a buzz but longer, and it goes on the longcar lanes. You know…?" The boy looked as puzzled as Sergeant Scott, to say nothing of accusing.

"No, I don't know!" The policeman shook his head, trying to control his frown. "A 'buzz'?" Scott could feel the first twinges of one of his bilious headaches coming on, and so decided to change the subject.

"What does your father do, son? He's a science-fiction writer, eh?— And you're next in a long line?"

"Dad's a snarker," the answer came quite spontaneously, without any visible attempt at deceit or even flippancy. In any case, the boy was obviously far too worried to be flippant. A "nut," Scott decided—but nevertheless a nut in trouble.

Now the kid had an inquisitive look on his face. "What's science fiction?" he asked.

"Science fiction," the big sergeant answered with feeling, "is that part of a policeman's lot called 'desk-duty'—when crazy lost kids walk into the station in tears to mess up said policeman's life!"

His answer set the youngster off worse than before.

Sighing, Scott passed his handkerchief across the desk and stood up. He called out to a constable in an adjacent room:

"Hey, Bob, come and look after the desk until Sergeant Healey gets in, will you? He's due on duty in the next ten minutes or so. I'll take the kid and see if I can find his father. If I can't—well, I'll bring the boy back here and the job can go through the usual channels."

"All right, Sergeant, I'll watch the shop," the constable agreed as he came into the duty-room and took his place at the desk. "I've been listening to your conversation! Right rum 'un that," he grinned, nodding towards the tearful boy. "What an imagination!"

Imagination, yes. And yet Scott was not quite sure. There was "something in the air," a feeling of impending—*strangeness*—hard to define.

"Come on, son," he said, shaking off his mood. "Let's go."

He took the boy's hand. "Let's see if we can find your dad. He's probably rushing about right now wondering what's become of you." He shook his head in feigned defeat and said: "I don't know—ten o'clock at night, just going off duty—and *you* have to walk in on me!"

"Ten o'clock—*already?*" The boy looked up into Scott's face with eyes wider and more frightened than ever. "Then we only have half an hour!

"Eh?" the policeman frowned again as they passed out into the London street (or was it "Mondon," Scott wondered with a mental grin). "Half an hour? What happens at half past ten, son? Do you turn into a pumpkin or something?" His humor was lost on his small charge.

"I mean the *lights!*" the boy answered, in what Scott took to be exasperation. "That's when the lights go out. At half past ten they put the lights out."

"They do?" the sergeant had given up trying to penetrate the boy's fertile but decidedly warped imagination. "Why's that, I wonder?" (Let the kid ramble on; it was better than tears at any rate.)

"Don't you know *anything?* the youngster seemed half-astonished, half-unbelieving, almost as if he thought Scott was pulling his leg.

"No," the sergeant returned, "I'm just a stupid copper! But come on—where did you give your father the slip? You said you passed Woolworths getting to the police station. Well, Woolworths is down this way, near the tube." He looked at the boy sharply in mistaken understanding. "You didn't get lost on the tube, did you? Lots of kids do when it's busy."

"The Tube?" Scott sensed that the youngster spoke the words in capitals—and yet it was only a whisper. He had to hold on tight as the boy strained away from him in something akin to horror. "No one goes down in the Tube anymore, except—" He shuddered.

"Yes?" Scott pressed, interested in this particular part of the boy's fantasy despite himself and the need, now, to have done with what would normally be a routine job. "Except who?"

"Not *who,*" the boy told him, clutching his hand tighter. "Not who, but—"

"But?" again, patiently, Scott prompted him.

"Not who but *what.*"

"Well, go on," said the sergeant, sighing, leading the way down the quiet, half-deserted street towards Woolworths. "*What,* er, goes down in the tube?"

"Why, Tubers, of course!" Again there was astonishment in the youngster's voice, amazement at Scott's obvious deficiency in general knowledge. "Aren't you Mondoners thick!" It was a statement of fact, not a question.

"Right," said Scott, not bothering to pursue the matter further, seeing the pointlessness of questioning an idiot. "We've passed Woolworths—now where?"

"Over there, I think, down that street. Yes!—that's where I lost my father—down there!"

"Come on," Scott said, leading the boy across the road, empty now of all but the occasional car, down into the entrance of the indicated street. In fact it was little more than an alley, dirty and unlighted. "What on earth were you doing down here in the first place?"

"We weren't down here," the youngster answered with a logic that made the sergeant's head spin. "We were in a bright street, with lots of lights. Then I felt a funny buzzing feeling, and...and then I was here! I got frightened and ran."

At that moment, their footsteps echoing hollowly on the cobbles of the alley, the sergeant felt a weird vibration that began in his feet and traveled up his body to his head, causing a burst of bright, painfully bilious stars to flash across his vision—and simultaneous with this peculiar sensation the two turned a corner to emerge with startling abruptness into a much brighter side street.

"That was the buzzing I told you about," the boy stated unnecessarily.

Scott was not listening. He was looking behind him for the broken electric cable he felt sure must be lying there just inside the alley (the sensation must surely have been caused by a mild electric shock), but he couldn't see one. Nor could he see anything else that might have explained that tingling, nerve-rasping sensation he had known. For that matter, where was the entrance (or exit) from which he and the boy had just this second emerged?

Where was the alley?

"Dad!" the kid yelled, suddenly tugging himself free to go racing off down the street.

Scott stood and watched, his head starting to throb and the street lights flaring garishly before his eyes. At the boy's cry a lone man had turned, started to run, and now Scott saw him sweep the lad up in his arms and wildly hug him, intense and obvious relief showing in his face.

The policeman forgot the problem of the vanishing alley and walked up to them, hands behind his back in the approved fashion, smiling benignly. "Cute lad you've got there, sir—but I should curb his imagination if I were you. Why, he's been telling me a story fit to—"

Then the benign smile slid from his face. "*Here!*" he cried, his jaw dropping in astonishment.

But despite his exclamation, Scott was nevertheless left standing on his own. For without a word of thanks both man and boy had made off down the street, hands linked, running as if the devil himself was after them!

"Here!" the policeman called again, louder. "Hold on a bit—"

For a moment the pair stopped and turned, then the man glanced at his watch (reminding Scott curiously of the White Rabbit in *Alice in*

Wonderland) before picking up the boy again and holding him close. "Get off the street!" he yelled back at Scott as he once more started to run. "Get off the streets, man." His white face glanced back and up at the street lights as he ran, and Scott saw absolute fear shining in his eyes. "It'll soon be half past ten!"

The policeman was still in the same position, his jaw hanging slack, some seconds later when the figure of the unknown man, again hugging the boy to him, vanished round a distant corner. Then he shrugged his shoulders and tried to pull himself together, setting his helmet more firmly on his aching head.

"Well I'll be—" He grinned nervously through the throb of his headache. "Snarker's son, indeed!"

Alone, now, Scott's feeling of impending—*something*—returned, and he noticed suddenly just how deserted the street was. He had never known London so quiet before. Why, there wasn't a single soul in sight!

And a funny thing, but here he was, only a stone's throw from his station, where he'd worked for the last fifteen years of his life, and yet— damned if he could recognize the street! Well, he knew he'd brought the boy down a dark, cobbled alley from the right, and so....

He took the first street on the right, walking quickly down it until he hit another street he knew somewhat better—

—Or did he?

Yes, yes, of course he did. The street was deserted now, quite empty, but just over there was good old....

Good old Wolwords!

Lights blazed and burst into multicolored sparks before Scott's bilious eyes. His mind spun wildly. He grabbed hold of a lamppost to steady himself and tried to think the thing out properly.

It must be a new building, that place—yes, that had to be the answer. He'd been doing a lot of desk-duties lately, after all. It was quite possible, what with new techniques and the speed of modern building, that the store had been put up in just a few weeks.

The place didn't *look* any too new, though....

Scott's condition rapidly grew worse—understandably in the circumstances, he believed—but there was a tube station nearby. He decided to take a train home. He usually walked the mile or so to his flat, the exercise did him good; but tonight he would take a train, give himself a rest.

He went dizzily down one flight of steps, barely noticing the absence of posters and the unkempt, dirty condition of the underground. Then, as he turned a corner, he came face-to-face with a strange legend, dripping in red paint on the tiled wall:

ROT THE TUBERS!

Deep creases furrowed the sergeant's forehead as he walked on, his footsteps ringing hollowly in the grimy, empty corridors, but his headache just wouldn't let him think clearly.

Tubers, indeed! What the hell—Tubers...?

Down another flight of steps he went, to the deserted ticket booths, where he paused to stare in disbelief at the naked walls of the place and the dirt- and refuse-littered floor. For the first time he really saw the *condition* of the place. What had happened here? Where was everyone?

From beyond the turnstiles he heard the rumble of a distant train and the spell lifted a little. He hurried forward then, past the empty booths and through the unguarded turnstiles, dizzily down one more flight of concrete steps, under an arch and out onto an empty platform. Not even a drunk or a tramp shared the place with him. The neons flared hideously, and he put out a hand against the naked wall for support.

Again, through the blinding flashes of light in his head, he noticed the absence of posters: the employment agencies, the pretty girls in lingerie, the film and play adverts, spectacular films and *avant-garde* productions—where in hell were they all?

Then, as for the first time he truly felt upon his spine the chill fingers of a slithering horror, there came the rumble and blast of air that announced the imminent arrival of a train—and he smelled the rushing reek of that which most certainly was *not* a train!

Even as he staggered to and fro on the unkempt platform, reeling under the fetid blast that engulfed him, the Tuber rushed from out its black hole—a *Thing* of crimson viscosity and rhythmically flickering cilia.

Sergeant Scott gave a wild shriek as a rushing feeler swept him from the platform and into the soft, hurtling plasticity of the thing—another shriek as he was whisked away into the deep tunnel and down into the bowels of the earth. And seconds later the minute hand of the clock above the empty, shuddering platform clicked down into the vertical position.

Ten-thirty—and all over Mondon, indeed throughout the length and breadth of Eenland, the lights went out.

★ ∴ ★

The Man
Who Felt Pain

First published in the excellent *Fantasy Tales* magazine
in the Spring 1989 issue, readers voted this next one the best of
the batch. "The Man Who Felt Pain" was written as a direct
result of my reading somewhere of the many seriously unpleas-
ant diseases that space-travel could bring about in astronauts.
Well naturally, being a writer of horror fiction, I at once recognized a sick but exciting little possibility that I felt I just had to
explore, and—

—But hey, that doesn't make me a bad person, does it?

BUT, YOU WOULD ASK, don't we all?

Yes, I would answer, we all feel pain—our own, and perhaps a little of
those who are closest to us—but rarely anyone else's. We don't physically
feel everyone else's pain. My twin brother, Andrew, felt everyone's pain, or
would have if he'd been able to bear it, but of course he couldn't and in the
end it killed him. Yes, and now it would kill me, too, except I intend to put
myself way, way beyond it.

So what do I mean, he could feel everyone's pain? Do I mean he was a
man of God, who felt *for* people? A man who agonized over all the world's
strife and turmoil, who felt the folly and frustration of men maiming and
killing each other in their petty squabbles and wars? Well, it's true he did,
to a certain extent, but no, that isn't what I mean.

I mean that he was the next leap forward in the evolution of the human
race. I mean that he was a member of time's tiny fraternity of genuine genius-
es, *sui generis* in fact, until the day he died. If he had happened on the shores
of some primal ocean, then he could have been the Missing Link; or five million years ago he might have been the first ape-man to use a branch to lever

rocks down in an avalanche upon his next meal; or a million years later employed fire to cook that meal; or just two million years ago used the first log 'wheels' to roll a megalith boulder to and fro across the entrance to his cave. They were all steps forward, and so was Andrew, except he was a leap.

For if we all felt everyone's pain, why, then there'd be no more wars or cruelties or hurtfulness of any sort and we could get on with the real business of our being here—which is to question *why* we're here, and to care for each other, and to go on...wherever.

I've thought about it a lot up here, where there's plenty of space and time to think, and my thoughts have been diverse.

There are these green bushes (I forget their name) which have oval leaves in tight, mathematically precise rows down their stems, and if you hold a burning match under one of them they all close up! And not only on that bush but on every other bush of that species in the vicinity! An intricate trigger mechanism created by Nature—or God, if you're a believer—and transmitted through sap and fiber, branch, twig, root and perhaps even soil; intricate and yet simple, if you know how. A card up the sleeve of...of a bush?

In the ocean there are polyps—organisms, occasionally huge, made up of tiny individual units each with lives of their own—which, when the predator fish bites one, the entire colony retracts into the safety of its alveolate rock or anchorage. Nature has allowed each to feel the agony of the others—for self-preservation. But to give such a gift to...a coral? A jellyfish? A polyp? If it could be done for such lowly creatures as these, why then create Man and simply leave him to his own devices? Surely that was to ask for trouble!

And so Andrew was the next step forward, for when he was born Nature also gave the gift to him. Except that I saw it in action and know that in fact it was a curse.

Now from up here I look down on the world revolving far below—at the beautiful green and blue planet Earth, which is slowly but surely destroying me—and while I remember almost exactly how it began, I daren't even think how it will end....

Our mother was American, our father English, and we were born in August 2027 at Lyon, France, where at that time could be found the Headquarters of ESP, the European Space Program. Our parents worked on the Program: she was and still is a computer technician, and he a PTI and instructor astronaut. He had journeyed into space many times during that decade in which we were born, but was forced to give it up when the technology got beyond him. A pity he never had Mother's mental wizardry, her computer-oriented brain. Anyway he has a desk job now, from which he'll retire, but reluctantly, in another five or six years' time.

I suppose it was only natural that Andrew and I should want to be astronauts; by the time Dad was finishing up we were already cramming maths and computer studies, aviation and astronautics, space flight subjects across the board. And, like the twins we were—like peas in a pod—we paralleled each other in performance. If I was top of the class one term, Andrew would pip me the next, and vice versa. At nineteen we flew the ESP shuttles (pilot and/or co-pilot, whichever task suited us at the time, or simply as crew-members) and at twenty-one we'd been to Moonbase and back. Always together.

The trouble started at Cannes, South of France, in the summer of 2049, when we were resting up after a month-long series of shuttle runs to destroy a lot of outdated space debris: sputs and sats and bits of old rockets lodged in their many, often dangerous orbits up there far outside Earth's envelope. I won't go into details, for any ten-year-old kid knows them: it was just a matter of giving these odd piles of freewheeling, obsolete junk a little shove in the right direction at the right time, to send them tumbling sadly and yet somehow grandly out and away and down into the hot heart of Sol.

But we were very young men and space is a lonely place, and so when we had our feet on the ground we liked to look for company. Nothing permanent, for we didn't lead the sort of life that makes for lasting relationships, but if you're an astronaut and can't find a little female company on a beach in Cannes…then it has to be time to see a plastic surgeon! On this occasion, however, we were on our own, just lying there on our towels on the beach and absorbing the heat of that especially hot summer, when it happened. I say 'it,' for at first we didn't know what it was. Not for quite some little time, in fact.

"Aaaah-*ow!*" said Andrew, abruptly sitting up and rapidly blinking his eyes, staring out across an entirely placid ocean. And though there was a twinge of pain in his voice he wasn't holding himself; he'd simply gone a little pale and shuddery, as if he had stomach cramp or something.

"Ow?" I repeated after him, but not quite, because the sound he'd made hadn't really been repeatable: more an animal cry than a word proper. "You were stung?" He frowned, looked at the sand all about, shook his head. "I…I don't think so," he finally, uncertainly, said.

I looked at him—at the physical fact and presence of my brother—in admiration, which was nice because I was looking at a better-than-mirror image of myself! Andrew, with his mass of gleaming black hair, blue eyes and clean, strong features, and his athlete's body. How many times had I wondered: *do I really look as good as this?*

But…a few minutes later and his stab of unknown pain was forgotten, and a spear-fisherman came out of the sea with a silver-glistening fish, shot through the head, stone dead on his spear. He took off his swimfins and marched proudly off up the beach with his catch. And Andrew's eyes followed him, still frowning. That was all there was to it, that first time.

After that the pains came thick and fast: big hurts and small ones, pains that made him burn or ache or sometimes simply cramped him, but occasionally agonies that doubled him over and caused him to throw up on the floor. None of them coming for any good reason that we could think of, and not a one from any visible cause or having any viable cure.

The Program medics all agreed that there was nothing wrong with Andrew, at least not with his body, and they were the best in the world and should know. But he and I, we knew that there was something desperately wrong with him. He was feeling pain, and feeling it when in fact he was in the peak of condition and nothing, absolutely *nothing*, should hurt.

I remember a fight in a night club in Paris; though we weren't involved personally, still I had to carry Andrew to our car and drive him to a friend's house. It was as though he was the one who took the hammering—and not a mark on him, and anyway the scrap had taken place on the other side of the room. But he'd certainly jerked upright out of his seat, grunting and yelling and slamming this way and that as the shouting and sounds of fists striking flesh reached us! And he'd just as surely crashed over on to his back on the floor, groggy as a punch-drunk ex-boxer, as the fight came to a close.

I remember the night in Lyon when he woke up hoarsely screaming his agony and clawing at his face. We were sleeping on the base at the time and there'd been some party or other we hadn't attended. But I'd heard the crash outside at the same time Andrew started yelling, and when I looked out of the window there was this accident down there, where a once-pretty girl had been tossed through a windscreen on to the hood of a second car, her face shattered and bloody. Andrew sat on his bed and moaned and shuddered and held his face together (which *was* together, you understand) until an ambulance came and took the injured girl away….

And that was when it finally began to dawn on us just what was wrong, and what was rapidly getting worse; so that it's hardly surprising he had his breakdown. He had it because he'd begun to realize that nothing and no one could ever put his problem right, and that from now on he was subject to anyone else's, everyone else's, pain.

For that was the simple fact of it: that he felt pain. From the pinprick stings of small, damaged or dying creatures to the screaming agonies of hideous human death. But once we knew what it was, at least we could tell the doctors.

It didn't take them long to check it out, and after they did…I've never seen so many intelligent down-to-earth men looking so downright shocked and disbelieving and lost for answers. And lost is the only word for it, for how can you treat someone for the aches and pains and bumps and cuts and bruises of someone else? How can you treat—or begin treating—the agony of a broken leg when the leg plainly isn't broken?

Non-addictive painkillers, obviously….

Oh, really?

For in fact it did no good to give painkillers to Andrew. The pain wasn't actually in him: its source or sources were beyond his mind and body; coming from outside of him, there was nothing they could put inside of him that would help. Worse, it didn't even bring relief when they gave the pills to the ones actually suffering from the pain! They only thought the pain had gone away, because it had been blocked. But the cause of the hurting was still there and Andrew could feel it….

The thing's progress was rapid; it precisely paralleled Andrew's deterioration. Obviously, he wasn't going out into space any more….

Or *was* he?

Once they'd accepted this new thing—Andrew's…disease?—the ESP medics were amenable to an idea of mine. And they backed me on it. For seven years we'd been using one-man weather sats for accurate forecasting. The robot sats had been fine in their day, but nothing was as clear-sighted as human eyes and nothing so observant as an alert human brain. And what with the extensive damage to the ozone layer—the constant fluctuation of its tears and holes—computer probability was at best mechanical guesswork anyway.

So—my idea was simple and I don't think I need to restate it. It would mean Andrew would be completely isolated for two months at a stretch, which isn't good for anyone, but at least it would give him time to get himself back together again before they brought him down for his periodic visits in hell. And it would also give the medics time to try to find a new angle of approach. Because if this was a disease connected with, or perhaps even springing from, space, then it was something they were going to have to take a crack at.

It took some haggling (the Program Chiefs like to have one hundred percent fit men up there), but between the medics, myself and my parents we convinced the upper echelon that Andrew should become WWO & A, a World Weather Observer & Adviser. And he and I spent another three months getting him back on his feet again, mentally and physically. Which wasn't easy.

It meant spending a lot of time in the loneliest places in the world: in deserts, on frozen ocean strands, in the wilds of Canada and blustery Scottish highlands, finally on the uninhabited beaches of Cyprus, which the deteriorating ozone layer had put paid to as far back as 2006. There weren't a hell of a lot of Venuses on half-shells floating ashore at Paphos this time around.

We talked and trained, and Andrew got himself together and faced up to it, and away from all the pains of men he gradually improved and became fit again. But at the same time he'd been growing ever more aware of a very worrying thing: the PE was wearing down. PE was our jargon for the ratio between a person in pain and his distance from Andrew, the receiver. The Proximity Effect. Previously, the source had needed to be pretty close. But now…all the world's pain, however muted, was getting there, was getting through to him. He felt it like you might hear the sea in a shell: as a distant tumult. A roaring which was gradually creeping up on him.

Nor was that the whole thing; for he'd also become more sensitive to the agonies of the smaller creatures, whose myriad ravages had grown that much more sharp to him. A huge cloud of desiccated, exhausted migratory butterflies spiraled down out of the aching Mediterranean sky to drown in the tideless sea, and Andrew gaped and gasped and began to turn blue before the last of them had expired. He felt the dull shuddering of the tiny clam devoured by the starfish, and the intolerable burning of the stranded man-o'-war evaporating on the sand. And now he couldn't get back into space fast enough.

Except…he never made it.

It was on every vidscreen in the world and dominated every newscast for a month: the blow-up at Fatu Hiva in the Marquesas.

There were two launches scheduled for that day. The first was a French relief team going up to Luna Orbital Station, and the second was supposed to be Andrew shuttling up to W-Sat III. But the French team never got off the pad, which meant that Andrew never got on it. We were only a mile away from that mess, waiting out the countdown when it fireballed—and my twin brother felt every poor sod of them frying! If they'd all gone up at once in the bang it would have been bad enough—but three of them, blazing, managed to eject. And Andrew blazed with them.

The medics took him back then, and called in the shrinks too, and I found myself excluded. Now it had to be up to the specialists, because I couldn't reach him any more. He'd gone "inside" and wasn't coming out for a while.

We were twins and I loved him; I might easily have gone to pieces myself, if the Old Folks had let me. But they didn't. "You've earned a lot of money, son, you and Andrew," my father told me. "Which is just as well because your brother is going to need it. Oh, I know, there are a lot of good people working on him for free—but there are other specialists who haven't even seen him yet, and they cost money. Money doesn't last for ever, Ray—it comes and it goes. If you want to do something for Andrew, want to take care of his future, then the best thing would be to get yourself back into space. Let me and your mother look after this end a while."

Andrew's future! It hadn't even got through to the Old Folks that he didn't have one. It was something they couldn't allow themselves to believe, and so they didn't. But at least their advice was good and kept me together. I went back into space, and up there where I could look down and see everything clearly (so clearly that I used to believe it allowed me to think more clearly, too) I'd sometimes wonder: why him and not me? *We're twins, so how come it skipped me?* But even in space there was no answer to that. Not then….

I did two months on W-Sat HI standing in for Andrew, and almost without pause a further three months on the vast, incredible wheel which was Luna Orbital, watching the EV engineers laboriously putting together the miracle that would one day become Titan Station. And finally it was back to Earth.

Meanwhile, I hadn't been out of touch: I got coded radio mail which my personal receiver unscrambled on to disks for me. The Old Folks kept me in the picture regarding Andrew.

"We found a specializing chemist who designed a drug for him," my mother told me, her languid American drawl still very much in evidence for all that she'd been expatriate for thirty years. "It has side-effects—makes his whole skin itch and upsets his balance a little—but it does cut down on the pain. And it's non-addictive!" Fine for anyone else; but my brother, my double, the athlete who was my twin? In private I cried about it.

"He's out of dock," the Old Man's gravelly English tones cheerfully informed me towards the end of one message, "house-hunting off Land's End!"

That last had me stumped. What the hell was "off" Land's End? I called up the atlas on my computer and got the answer: the Isles of Scilly. But it was the wrong answer. There were also several lighthouses.

When I got back down I had three months' accumulated R and R and plenty to do with it, but first the Program Officer I/C wanted to see me. In Lyon I went up to Jean-Pierre Durant's office and was ushered in. Durant was a short, sturdy man in his fifties, wide as a door, short-cropped graying hair, big hard hands, very powerful looking. And he was powerful in every way; but big-hearted with it, a man who loved his fellow men. Right then, however, I had a down on ESP because of Andrew (to me, they'd seemed too eager to write him off) and possibly it showed in my face. Also, I was in a hurry to get across the Channel to England, and down to Land's End, and out to see my brother in the old deserted lighthouse he'd made his home. So Durant was the Big Boss—so what? I considered this an intrusion into my time. And perhaps that showed, too.

"Sit down, Ray," Durant invited, smiling, waving me into a chair. He spoke English which his accent made warm and compassionate, salving a little of the anger and frustration out of me. "And don't worry," he continued, "I don't intend to waste your time. I'll get right down to it: we think there's maybe something we can do for Andrew—if it's at all possible."

My heart gave a leap and I started to my feet again. "The medics have come up with something?"

Durant shook his head, pointed at the chair. Frowning, I sat. "The psychoanalysts!" I burst out again, leaning forward. "It was psychosomatic, right? Some kind of mental allergy?"

"Ray," he said, again shaking his head, "they're working on those things—and getting nowhere fast. And Andrew isn't helping by making it hard for anyone to see him. So…we're not making much progress. Not along those lines, anyway."

I was still frowning. "So how can you help him?"

Durant looked tugged two ways; he sighed, shrugged, stroked his chin. "Personally, I think he should go back out into space again."

I stared at him for a moment, then slumped. "We tried that," I said, disappointed.

He ignored my expression and my answer, and said: "Way out in space." But it was *how* he said it. This time there was no way I could remain seated: I jumped up, leaned forward across his desk. If Durant meant what I thought he meant…it had always been our wildest dream!

"Titan?" I finally got it out.

He nodded, and repeated himself: "*Way* out! Far beyond the influence of whatever it is that's killing him. If we can get him up to Moonbase for a year…we think we may have the Titan hardware ready by then. You've been up on the Luna Orbiter and know how hard they're all working up there. The Titan wheel was going to be unmanned at first, as you know, with its life-supports on green just waiting for a crew when we were ready to send them. However—" And he smiled again, and shrugged.

I took a pace back, collapsed into my chair, dazedly shook my head as a mixture of emotions flooded through me. "But…why tell me? I mean, haven't you told Andrew?"

Now the smile, a worried one at best, left his face. "I told him last week—by letter, special delivery, a jet copter—and his answer…wasn't satisfactory. I told him yesterday, and when he could bring himself to answer the phone I got the same response. And I've tried to tell him again this morning, but apparently he's not taking calls. So maybe you'd better tell him for me."

"Unsatisfactory?" Over everything else he'd said that one word had stuck in my mind. "His answer was unsatisfactory? In what way?"

"Ray," Durant looked straight into my eyes, "your brother is convinced he's going to die—of other people's pain. He says he's given it plenty of thought and knows there's no way of stopping it. And he says that since it's coming, he'd prefer it came here on Earth than out there. Going out into space would only delay it anyway, he says. So you're his last chance. Possibly he's already too far gone physically for the job, in which case you'll not only have to talk him into accepting it, but also get him back up on his feet one last time. You did it before, between you, so maybe you can do it again. That's the whole thing, and that's why I sent for you…."

"Do my parents—?" I started, but he cut me off.

"Your parents are your parents, Ray. I know them almost as well as you do. In some respects I know them better. Andrew has forbidden them to visit him, says not to baby him and that he's doing fine, and when he's ready to see them he'll turn up on their doorstep. Do you think it's likely—or even right—that I should tell them he's going downhill? But I have told them we *might* send him out to Saturn if he wants it, and that it's up to him. Though in fact it now looks like it's up to you. When are you seeing him?"

"Tomorrow," I said. "As soon as I can get there. Right now, if there was any quick way."

"There is," he told me. "Get your things together, whatever you want to take with you, and be at the helipad in one hour. I'll clear it and see that you're jet-coptered over. Two and a half hours and you're there, OK?"

And of course I said yes, that was OK….

I didn't try to call Andrew first; it was to be a surprise, and it was. But on the way across I talked to my pilot, the one who'd taken Durant's letter to Andrew on Perring's Rock. "How did he look to you?" I asked him.

Josh Bertin was a Belgian and had been a jet-copter pilot for ESP as long as I'd been around; I knew him personally and he knew our history. "Andrew…wasn't his brightest," he answered, carefully. And, before I could quiz him further: "You know why he bought the Rock, of course?"

"Oh, yes," I nodded. "Miles out to sea. No people. No pain. Not so much, anyway."

Josh glanced at me out of the corner of his eye. "Yes…and no," he said. "Oh, that's the reason he settled there, for sure, but—"

When his pause threatened to go on indefinitely, I prompted him: "But?"

"He mentioned something you and he call the PE? Something to do with how close people were to him? Well, he told me it's breaking down. All the way down."

"Josh," I was really alarmed now, "I think you'd better tell me—"

"*But*," he broke in on me, "he's coping with it—so far. Learning to live with it. All he has to do is keep telling himself it's not real, that's all—that the pain belongs to someone else—and then he'll be OK. As long as nothing big happens. But right out there in the sea? Well, he's not expecting any disasters, you know? And Ray, that's it. No good asking me any more, 'cos that's all he told me."

I said nothing but simply turned over what he'd said in my mind. And while I was still turning it over, that's when the pain hit me. Andrew's pain—and I knew it!

It came from outside of me, slamming into me like an explosive shell and fragmenting deep inside. It was like a tankful of pain had overflowed into my guts. Someone was crushing my heart, yanking it this way and that, trying to tear it out of me. I had thought I knew what pain was, but I hadn't. *This* was pain! Big Pain!

It would have driven me surging to my feet, but I was strapped in. I cried out, or gurgled, and then I must have blacked out….

When I came to Josh had slapped an oxygen mask over my nose and mouth and was shaking me. He'd switched the jet-copter to automatic pilot, and he was white as death. But as soon as I opened my eyes, dragged the mask off my face and let it fall, then he took a deep breath and climbed down a little. "Are you OK?" he said. And: "Jesus, Ray—what was all *that*?"

At the time I'd known what it was, but now I couldn't be sure, didn't want to be sure. I had thought it was Andrew, something from him that couldn't be contained, overflowing into me. But…I didn't even know if that was possible. Being a twin, I knew all about the so-called "Corsican Brothers" case, but nothing like that had ever happened to me (to us?) before. So…maybe it was just me. My heart? Had I been pushing it too hard?

"I don't know what it was," I finally answered Josh. "I'm too scared to *think* what it was. I only know it was pain, and that it's gone now."

But I didn't tell him that something else had gone, too, something which I hadn't even been aware of until suddenly—right there and then— I no longer had it. It had been a warm feeling, that's all. A feeling that there was something out there other than what I could see, feel and touch. A sure knowledge that the universe was bigger than me. Now that I'd lost it I knew that it had been something greater than merely "I think, therefore I am." Perhaps it had been "we think…." But now there was just an empti-ness, with nothing out there at all except the world and all of space and all the other stars and worlds in it. And for the first time in my life I experienced loneliness. Even with someone right there beside me, I was lonely….

It was mid-September, still warm but very soggy, and fog lay like a milky shroud on the ocean where Perring's Rock stuck up like a partly clenched fist from the grey surging water, its lighthouse index finger point-ing at the leaden sky. Perring's Rock was the sloping acre and a half plateau of some drowned mountain, rising seventy or eighty feet out of the sea with the lighthouse built at the highest point of the slope. There was some-thing of a tiny scalloped bay and beach to the west, away from our approach path, and a flat area on our side of the lighthouse picked out with typical helipad patterns.

Like ninety per cent of all lighthouses the Rock had been abandoned since before the turn of the century, when super high-tech Radar, Skyspy and the W-sats had put them out of business for good. But the way they'd built this one, the sea wasn't going to claim it for a long time still to come. And desolate? The place looked about as lonely as I now felt. Except as we landed I saw that it wasn't, or saw something which caused me to think that it wasn't.

It was Andrew himself!—leaning over the rail of the lighthouse's cir-cular balcony or platform, waving to us through the blast from our fans as we came down. Then I was free of my straps and sliding the cabin door open, out of my seat and down under the rotors before they'd even nearly stopped turning, and running up the rock-carved steps to pause at the foot of the tower. And there was my brother up top, still leaning on the rail high overhead, his shirt-sleeves flapping in a breeze sprung up off the sea. Except…he wasn't looking down at me at all but at something else. And he was so still, so very still there at the rail. Not so much leaning on it, I now saw, as propped up by it.

I was inside and up the steps three at a time; and no need to worry now about the state of my heart for I was galvanized, my actions electric, supercharged! Yanked aloft by a fear and a pain beyond physical pain, I hurtled up those steps, while from behind and below me Josh Bertin's cry followed despairingly from the well of the corkscrew: "Ray!…Ray…!'

Up to the old lamp room I swept, and on up its iron ladder and through the open trapdoor on to the flat, circular roof. And there was Andrew clinging to the iron three-bar safety rail—or rather hanging on it. One foot had slipped through and jammed there, dangling in space, and the other leg was bent at the knee, propping him against an upright. His left arm lay loosely along the top rail, while his opposite shoulder and arm lolled stiffly across it, supporting his weight. With his shirt-sleeves flapping like that and his head on one side, he looked like…like a sorry scarecrow fallen from its cross. And I saw that I was right and he hadn't in fact been looking at us as we came in but at something else, down on the beach—as he'd blindly stared at it ever since his final, killing pain had reached out to me and knocked me out during the flight.

The mist had curled away a little and now I too could see it there on the narrow shingle strand. A beached whale, with three great, deep crimson slashes across its spine where some liner's screw had broken its broad back!

The blood was still pumping, though very sluggishly now, sporadically; overhead the gulls wheeled and cried their excitement, like vultures waiting for the last spark to flicker low and expire; out at sea a cow and her calf stood off and spouted, and it seemed to me that over and above my own pain I could feel something of theirs, too.

…Until, like ice-water down my back, there dawned the realization that *I could actually feel it*, and finally I knew that I was compensating for Andrew's loss….

That was three months ago and since then…I've thought about it a lot up here, where there's plenty of time and space to think. And my thoughts have been diverse.

I watch the curving reef which is Japan appear at the rim of the mighty Pacific, and as it slides closer I can point a trembling finger at the very bay where in these same moments of time the dolphins are still being slaughtered in their thousands. I feel the outward rush of human agony as bombs explode in Zambia, while the African continent slips by so distantly beneath my observation ports that my eyes see nothing but its beauty. A million babies are born and their mothers cry out, and a million men die—but they only feel their own pain while I feel something of all of it. And with every revolution I feel more.

Nine months to go, and Saturn is waiting for me out there beyond the pain of the world. But now and then I ask myself: will the wash from the world one day reach out to me even there? Or will I have moved on, outwards to the stars, before then?

Sometimes I wonder: are there other men or beings out there, in the stars?

And sometimes I pray there are not….

★ ✱ ★

The Strange Years

Seven years before "The Man Who Felt Pain," this next story had also made its debut in *Fantasy Tales* (Spring, 1982). Now, I've always had a weird fascination for the *Attack of the* What-the-Hell-Ever subgenre of stories, whether it's body-snatchers or fifty-foot women or killer tomatoes, so sooner or later I knew I was going to have to have a go at it too. And let's face it, there had been some very strange years in the late 1970s. Anyway, Steve Jones—one of the editors and the guiding light of England's most prestigious, best-remembered fantastic magazine at that time—Steve called "The Strange Years" "an apocalyptic jewel," about which I was well pleased. But the story may even in its way have been a little prophetic, too. Because truth to tell there's been some even stranger, far more malicious years since....

HE LAY FACE-DOWN on the beach at the foot of a small dune, his face turned to one side, the summer sun beating down upon him. The clump of beachgrass at the top of the dune bent its spikes in a stiff breeze, but down here all was calm, with not even a seagull's cry to break in upon the lulling *hush, hush* of waves from far down the beach.

It would be nice, he thought, to run down the beach and splash in the sea, and come back dripping salt water and tasting it on his lips, and for the very briefest of moments be a small boy again in a world with a future. But the sun beat down from a blue sky and his limbs were leaden, and a great drowsiness was upon him.

Then...a disturbance. Blown on the breeze to climb the far side of the dune, flapping like a bird with broken wings, a slim book—a child's exercise book, with tables of weights and measures on the back—flopped down exhausted in the sand before his eyes. Disinterested, he found strength to push it away; but as his fingers touched it so its cover blew open to reveal pages written in a neat if shaky adult longhand.

He had nothing else to do, and so began to read....

"When did it begin? Where? How? Why?

"The Martians we might have expected (they've been frightening us long enough with their tales of invasion from outer space) and certainly there have been enough of threats from our Comrades across the water. But this?

"Any ordinary sort of plague, we would survive. We always have in the past. And as for war: Christ!—when has there not been a war going on somewhere? They've irradiated us in Japan, defoliated us in Vietnam, smothered us in DDT wherever we were arable and poured poison into us where we once flowed sweet and clean—and we always bounced right back.

"Fire and flood—even nuclear fire and festering effluent—have not appreciably stopped us. For 'They' read 'We,' Man, and for 'Us' read 'the world,' this Earth which once was ours. Yes, there have been strange years, but never a one as strange as this.

"A penance? The ultimate penance? Or has Old Ma Nature finally decided to give us a hand? Perhaps she's stood off, watching us try our damnedest for so damned long to exterminate ourselves, and now She's sick to death of the whole damned scene. 'OK,' She says, 'have it your own way.' And She gives the nod to Her Brother, the Old Boy with the scythe. And He sighs and steps forward, and—

"And it is a plague of sorts; and certainly it is DOOM; and a fire that rages across the world and devours all...Or will that come later? The cleansing flame from which Life's bright phoenix shall rise again? There will always be the sea. And how many ages this time before something gets left by the tide, grows lungs, jumps up on its feet and walks...and reaches for a club?

"*When* did it begin?

"I remember an Irish stoker who came into a bar dirty and drunk. His sleeves were rolled up and he scratched at hairy arms. I thought it was the heat. 'Hot? Damned right, sur,' he said, 'an' hotter by far down below—an' lousy!' He unrolled a newspaper on the bar and vigorously brushed at his matted forearm. Things fell onto the newsprint and moved, slowly. He popped them with a cigarette. "'Crabs, sur!' he cried. 'An' Christ!—they suck like crazy!'

"*When?*

"There have always been strange years—plague years, drought years, war and wonder years—so it's difficult to pin it down. But the last twenty years…they have been *strange*. When, *exactly*! Who can say? But let's give it a shot. Let's start with the 70s—say, '76?—the drought.

"There was so little water in the Thames that they said the river was running backwards. The militants blamed the Soviets. New laws were introduced to conserve water. People were taken to court for watering flowers. Some idiot calculated that a pound of excreta could be satisfactorily washed away with six pints of water, and people put bricks in their WC cisterns. Someone else said you could bathe comfortably in four inches of water, and if you didn't use soap the resultant mud could be thrown on the garden. The thing snowballed into a national campaign to 'Save It!'—and in October the skies were still cloudless, the earth parched, and imported rainmakers danced and pounded their tom-toms at Stonehenge. Forest and heath fires were daily occurrences and reservoirs became dustbowls. Sun-worshippers drank Coke and turned very brown….

"And finally it rained, and it rained, and it rained. Wide-spread flooding, rivers bursting their banks, gardens (deprived all summer) inundated and washed away. Millions of tons of water, and not a pound of excreta to be disposed of. A strange year, '76. And just about every year since, come to think.

"'77, and stories leak out of the Ukraine of fifty thousand square miles turned brown and utterly barren in the space of a single week. Since then the spread has been very slow, but it hasn't stopped. The Russians blamed 'us' and we accused 'them' of testing a secret weapon.

"'79 and '80, and oil tankers sinking or grounding themselves left, right and center. Miles-long oil slicks and chemicals jettisoned at sea, and whales washed up on the beaches, and Greenpeace, and the Japanese slaughtering dolphins. Another drought, this time in Australia, and a plague of mice to boot. Some Aussie commenting that 'The poor 'roos are dying in their thousands—and a few aboes, too….' And great green swarms of aphids and the skies bright with ladybirds.

"Lots of plagues, in fact. We were being warned, you see?

"And '84! Ah—1984! Good old George!

"He was wrong, of course, for it wasn't Big Brother at all. It was Big Sister—Ma Nature Herself. And in 1984 She really started to go off the rails. '84 was half of India eaten by locusts and all of Africa down with a mutant strain of beriberi. '84 was the year of the poisoned potatoes and sinistral periwinkles, the year it rained frogs over wide areas of France, the year the cane-pest shot sugar beet right up to the top of the crops.

"And not only Ma Nature but Technology, too, came unstuck in '84. The Lake District chemically polluted—permanently; nuclear power stations at Loch Torr on one side of the Atlantic and Long Island on the other melting down almost simultaneously; the Americans bringing back a 'bug' from Mars (see, even a *real* Martian invasion); oil discovered in the Mediterranean, and new fast-drilling techniques cracking the ocean floor and allowing it to leak and leak and leak—and even Red Adair shaking his head in dismay. How do you plug a leak two hundred fathoms deep and a mile long? And that jewel of oceans turning black, and Cyprus a great white tombstone in a lake of pitch. 'Aphrodite Rising From The High-Grade.'

"Then '85 and '86; and they were strange, too, because they were so damned quiet! The lull before the storm, so to speak. And then—

"Then it was '87, '88 and '89. The American space-bug leaping to Australia and New Zealand and giving both places a monstrous malaise. No one doing any work for six months; cattle and sheep dead in their millions; entire cities and towns burning down because nobody bothered to call out the fire services, or they didn't bother to come…. And all the world's beaches strewn with countless myriads of great dead octopuses, a new species (or a mutant strain) with three rows of suckers to each tentacle; and their stink utterly unbearable as they rotted. A plague of great, fat seagulls. All the major volcanoes erupting in unison. Meteoric debris making massive holes in the ionosphere. A new killer cancer caused by sunburn. The common cold cured!—and uncommon leprosy spreading like wildfire through the Western World.

"And finally—

"Well, that was 'When.' It was also, I fancy, 'Where' and 'How.' As to 'Why'—I give a mental shrug. I'm tired, probably hungry. I have some sort of lethargy—the spacebug, 1 suppose—and I reckon it won't be long now. I had hoped that getting this down on paper might keep me active, mentally if not physically. But….

"*Why?*

"Well, I think I've answered that one, too.

"Ma Nature strikes back. Get rid of the human vermin. They're lousing up your planet! And maybe *that's* what gave Her the idea. If fire and flood and disease and disaster and war couldn't do the trick, well, what else could She do? They advise you to fight fire with fire, so why not vermin with vermin?"

"They appeared almost overnight, five times larger than their immediate progenitors and growing bigger with each successive hatching; and unlike the new octopus they didn't die; and their incubation period down to less than a week. The superlice. All Man's little body parasites, all of his tiny, personal vampires, growing in the space of a month to things as big as your fist. Leaping things, flying things, walking sideways things. To quote a certain Irishman: 'An' Christ—they suck like crazy!'

"They've sucked, all right. They've sucked the world to death. New habits, new protections—new immunities and near-invulnerability—to go with their new size and strength. The meek inheriting the Earth? Stamp on them and they scurry away. Spray them with lethal chemicals and they bathe in them. Feed them DDT and they develop a taste for it. 'An' Christ—they suck like crazy!'

"And the whole world down with the creeping, sleeping sickness. We didn't even *want* to fight them! Vampires, and they've learned new tricks. Camouflage…. Clinging to walls above doors, they look like bricks or tiles. And when you go through the door…. And their bite acts like a sort of LSD. Brings on mild hallucinations, a feeling of well-being, a kind of euphoria. In the cities, amongst the young, there were huge gangs of 'bug-people!' My God!

"They use animals, too; dogs and cats—as mounts, to get them about when they're bloated. Oh, they kill them eventually, but they know how to use them first. Dogs can dig under walls and fences; cats can climb and squeeze through tiny openings; crows and other large birds can fly down on top of things and into places….

"Me, I was lucky—if you can call it that. A bachelor, two dogs, a parakeet and an outdoor aviary. My bungalow entirely netted in; fine wire netting, with trees, trellises and vines. And best of all situated on a wild stretch of the coast, away from mankind's great masses. But even so, it was only a matter of time.

"They came, found me, sat outside my house, outside the wire and the walls, and they waited. They found ways in. Dogs dug holes for them, seagulls tore at the mesh overhead. Frantically, I would trap, pour petrol, burn, listen to them pop! But I couldn't stay awake for ever. One by one they got the birds, leaving little empty bodies and bunches of feathers. And my dogs, Bill and Ben, which I had to shoot and burn. And this morning when I woke up, Peter parakeet.

"So there's at least one of them, probably two or three, here in the room with me right now. Hiding, waiting for night. Waiting for me to go to sleep. I've looked for them, of course, but—

"Chameleons, they fit perfectly into any background. When I move, they move. And they imitate perfectly. But they do make mistakes. A moment ago I had two hairbrushes, identical, and I only ever had one. Can you imagine brushing your hair with something like *that*? And what the hell would I want with *three* fluffy slippers? A left, a right—and a center?

"…I can see the beach from my window. And half a mile away, on the point, there's Carter's grocery. Not a crust in the kitchen. Dare I chance it? Do I want to? Let's see, now. Biscuits, coffee, powdered milk, canned beans, potatoes—no, strike the potatoes. A sack of carrots…."

The man on the beach grinned mirthlessly, white lips drawing back from his teeth and freezing there. A year ago he would have expected to read such in a book of horror fiction. But not now. Not when it was written in his own hand.

The breeze changed direction, blew on him, and the sand began to drift against his side. It blew in his eyes, glazed now and lifeless. The shadows lengthened as the sun started to dip down behind the dunes. His body grew cold.

Three hairy sacks with pincer feet, big as footballs and heavy with his blood, crawled slowly away from him along the beach….

No Way Home

Like "Snarker's Son"—but very unlike it, too—"No Way Home" is a parallel universe story, first published in the prestigious *Magazine of Fantasy & Science Fiction (F&SF)* in September of 1975. I was still a serving soldier and had recently spent time back in the UK on leave (furlough). But many of the highways seemed to have been extended, rerouted, changed— some of them even appeared to have mutated!—while I'd been out of the country. Also, I was used to driving on the right-hand side of the road and back in the UK I was driving on the left again; or maybe I was just tired out and not taking enough care reading the road signs. Whatever, the fact is I'd gone and got myself lost. Now how in *hell* can you get lost in your own backyard? Well, actually it's easy—even in your own backyard—and easier still in hell....

IF YOU MOTOR UP the Ml past Lanchester from London and come off before Bankhead heading west across the country, within a very few miles you enter an area of gently rolling green hills, winding country roads and Olde Worlde villages with quaint wooden-beamed street-corner pubs and noonday cats atop leaning ivied walls. The roads there are narrow, climbing gently up and ribboning back down the green hills, rolling between fields, meandering casually through woods and over brick- and wooden-bridged streams; the whole background forms a pattern of peace and tranquility rarely disturbed over the centuries.

By night, though, the place takes on a different aspect. An almost miasmal aura of timelessness, of antiquity, hangs over the brooding woods and dark hamlets. The moon silvers winding hedgerows and ancient thatched roofs, and when the pubs close and the last lights blink out in farm and cottage windows, then it is as if Night had thrown her blackest cloak over the land, when even the most powerful headlight's beam penetrates the resultant darkness only with difficulty. Enough to allow you to drive on the narrower roads, if you drive slowly and carefully.

Strangers motoring through this region—even in daylight hours—are known occasionally to lose their way, to drive the same labyrinthine lanes for hours on end in meaningless circles. The contours of the countryside often seem to defy even the most accurate sense of direction, and the roads and tracks never quite seem to tally with printed maps of the area. There are rumors almost as old as the area itself that persons have been known to pass into oblivion here—like gray smoke from cottage chimneystacks disappearing into air—never to come out again.

Not that George Benson was a stranger. True, he had not been home to England for many years—since running off as a youth, later to marry and settle in Germany—but as a boy he had known this place well and must have cycled for thousands of miles along dusty summer roads, lanes and tracks, even bridle-paths through the heart of this very region.

And that was why he was so perturbed now: not because of a pack of lies and fairy stories and old wives' tales heard as a boy, but because this was his home territory, where he'd been born and reared. Indeed, he felt more than perturbed, stupid almost. A fellow drives all the way north through Germany from Dortmund, catches the car ferry from Bremerhaven into Harwich, rolls on up-country having made the transition from right- to left-of-the-road driving with only a very small effort.... and then hopelessly loses himself within only a fistful of miles from home!

Anger at his own supposed stupidity turned to bitter memories of his wife, then to an even greater anger. And a hurt....

It didn't hurt half so much now, though, not now that it was all over. But the anger was still there. And the memories of the milk of marriage gone sour. Greta had just upped and left home one day. George, employing the services of a detective agency, had traced his wife to Hamburg, where he'd found her in the bed of a nightclub crooner, an old boyfriend who finally had made it good.

"Damn all Krauts!" George cursed now as he checked the speed of his car to read out the legend on a village signpost. His headlights picked the letters out starkly in the surrounding darkness. "Middle Hamborough?—Never bloody heard of it!" Again he cursed as, making a quick decision, he spun the steering wheel to turn his big car about on the narrow road. He would have to start back-tracking, something he hated doing because it seemed so inefficient, so wasteful. "And blast and damn all Kraut cars!" he added as his front wheels bounced jarringly on to and back off the high stone roadside curb.

"Greta!" he quietly growled to himself as he drove back down the road away from the outskirts of Middle Hamborough. "What a *bitch*!" For of course she had blamed him for their troubles, saying that she couldn't stand his meanness. *Him*, George Benson, mean! She simply hadn't appreciated money. She'd thought that Deutschmarks grew on trees, that pfennigs gathered like dew on the grass in the night. George, on the other hand, had inherited many of the pecuniary instincts of his father, a Yorkshireman of the Old School—and of Scottish stock to boot—who really understood the value of "brass." His old man had used to say: "Thee tak' care o' the pennies, Georgie, an' the pounds'll tak' care o' theysels!"

George's already pinched face tightened skull-like as his thoughts again returned to Greta. She had wanted children. Children! Damned lucky thing he had known better than to accept that! For God's sake, who could afford children?

Then she'd complained about the food—like she'd been complaining for years—saying that she was getting thin because the money he gave her was never enough. But George liked his women willowy and fragile; that way there was never much fight in them.

Well, he'd certainly misjudged Greta, there had been plenty of fight left in her. And their very last fight had been about food, too. He had wanted her to buy food in bulk at the supermarkets for cheapness; in turn she'd demanded a deep freezer so that the food she bought wouldn't go bad; finally George had gone off the deep end when she told him how much the freezer she had in mind would cost!

She left him that same day; moreover, she ate the last of the wurstchen before she went! George grinned mirthlessly as he gripped the steering wheel tighter, wishing it were Greta's scrawny neck. By God—she'd be sorry when she was fat!

Still, George had had the last laugh. Their home had been paid for fifty-fifty, but it had been in George's name. He had sold it; likewise the furniture and the few clothes she'd left behind. The car had been half hers, too—but again in George's name, for Greta couldn't drive. It was all his now: his money, his car, everything. As he'd done so often in the last twenty-four hours, he took one hand from the wheel to pat reassuringly the fat wallet where its outline bulged out the upper right front pocket of his jacket.

It was the thought of money that sent George's mind casting back an hour or so to a chance encounter at Harvey's All-Night-Grill, just off the

Ml. This drunk had been there—oh, a real joker, and melancholy with it, too—but he had been so well-heeled! George remembered the man's queer offer: "Just show me the way home, that's all—and all I've got you can have!" And he had carried a checkbook showing a credit of over two thousand pounds....

That last was hearsay, though, passed on to George by Harvey himself, the stubble-jawed, greasy-aproned owner of the place. Now that earlier accidental meeting and conversation suddenly jumped up crystal clear in George's mind.

It had started when George mentioned to Harvey that he was heading for Bellington; that was when the other fellow had started to take an interest in him and had made his weird offer about being shown the way home.

God damn! George sat bolt upright behind the steering wheel. Come to think of it, he had heard of Middle Hamborough before. Surely that was the name of the place the drunk had been looking for—for fifteen years!

George hadn't paid much attention to the man at the time, had barely listened to his gabbled, drunken pleading. He'd passed the fellow off quite simply as some nut who'd heard those fanciful old rumors about people getting lost in the surrounding countryside, a drunk who was making a big play of his own personal little fantasy. He would be all right when he sobered up.

Now that George thought about it, though—well, why should anyone make up a story like that? And, come to think of it, the man hadn't seemed all that drunk. More tired and, well, lost, really....

Just then, cresting a low hill, as his headlights flashed across the next shallow valley, George saw the house with the big garden and the long drive winding up to it. The place stood to the right of the road, atop the next hill, and the gravel drive rose up from an ornamental stone arch and iron gate at the roadside. Dipping down the road and climbing the low hill, George read the wrought-iron legend on the gate: HIGH HOUSE. And now he remembered more of the—drunk's?—story.

The man had called himself Kent, and fifteen years ago, on his tenth wedding anniversary, he'd left home one morning to drive to London, there to make certain business arrangements with city-dwelling colleagues. He had taken a fairly large sum of money with him when he drove from High House, the home he himself had designed and built, and this had worked out just as well for him. Turning right off the Middle Hamborough road through Meadington and on to the London road at Bankhead, Kent had driven to the city. And in London—

Kent was a partner in a building concern with head offices in the city…or at least he had been. For in London he discovered that the firm had never existed, that his colleagues, Milton and Jones, while they themselves were real enough, swore they had never heard of him. "Milton, Jones & Kent" did not exist; the firm was known simply as "Milton & Jones." Not only did they not know him, they tried to have him jailed for attempted fraud!

That was only the start of it, for the real horror came when he tried to get back home—only to discover that there just wasn't any way home! George now remembered Kent's apparently drunken phrase: "A strange dislocation of space and time, a crossing of probability tracks, a passage between parallel dimensions—and a subsequent *snapping-back* of space-time elastic…." Now surely only a drunk would say something like that? A drunk or a nut. Except Harvey had insisted that Kent was sober. He was just tired, Harvey said, confused, half mad trying to solve a fifteen-year-old problem that wasn't. There had never been a Middle Hamborough, Harvey insisted. The place wasn't shown on any map; you couldn't find it in the telephone directory; no trains, buses, or roads went there. Middle Hamborough wasn't!

But Middle Hamborough *was*, George had seen it, or—

Could it be that greasy old Harvey had somehow been fooling that clown all these years, milking his money drop by drop, cashing in on some mental block or other? Or had they both simply been pulling George's leg? If so, well, it certainly seemed a queer sort of joke….

George glanced at his watch. Just 11:00 p.m. Damn it, he'd planned to be in Bellington by now, at home with the Old Folks, and he would have been if he'd come off the Ml at the right place.

Of course, when he'd left England there had been no motorway as such, just another road stretching away north and south. That was where he'd gone wrong; obviously he'd come off the Ml too soon. He should have gone on to the next exit. Well, all right, he'd kill two birds with one stone. He'd go back to Harvey's all-nighter, check out the weird one's story again, then see if he couldn't perhaps latch on to some of the joker's small change to cover his time. Then he'd try to pick up a map of the area before heading home. He couldn't go wrong with a map—now could he?

Having decided his course, and considering the winding roads and pitch darkness, George put his foot down and sped back to Harvey's place. Parking his car, he walked in through the open door into the unhealthy atmosphere and lighting of the so-called cafeteria (where the lights were kept low, George suspected, to make the young cockroaches on the walls less conspicuous). He went straight to the service counter and carefully rested his elbows upon it, avoiding the splashes of sticky coffee and spilled grease. Of the equally greasy proprietor he casually inquired the whereabouts of Mr. Kent.

"Eh? Kent? He'll be in his room. I let him lodge here, y'know. He doesn't like to be too far from this area...."

"You *let* him lodge here?" George asked, raising his eyebrows questioningly.

"Well, y'know—he pays a bit."

George nodded, silently repeating the other's words: Yeah, I'll *bet* he pays a bit!

"G'night there!" Harvey waved a stained dishcloth at a departing truck driver and his mate. "See y'next time." He turned back to George with a scowl. "Anyway, what's it to you, about Kent? After making y'self a quick quid or two?"

"How do you mean?" George returned, assuming a hurt look. "It's just that I think I might be able to help the poor bloke out, that's all."

"Oh?" Harvey looked suspicious. "How's that, then?"

"Well, half an hour ago I was on the road to Middle Hamborough, and I passed a place set back off the road called High House. I just thought—"

"'Ere," Harvey cut in, a surprisingly fast hand shooting out to catch George's jacket front and pull him close so that their faces almost met across the service counter. "You tryin' t' be clever, chief?"

"Well, I'll be—" George spluttered, genuinely astonished. "What the hell do you think you're—'

"Cos if you are—you an' me'll fall out, we will!"

George carefully disengaged himself. "Well," he said, "I think that answers one of my questions, at least."

"Eh? What d'you mean?' Harvey asked, still looking surly. George backed off a step.

"Looks to me like you're as mad as him, attacking me like that. I mean, I might have expected you to laugh, seeing as how I fell for your funny little joke—but I'd hardly think you'd get all physical."

"What the merry 'ell are you on about?" Harvey questioned, a very convincing frown creasing his forehead. "What joke?"

"Why, about Middle Hamborough, about it not being on any map and about no roads going there and Kent looking for the place for fifteen years. I'm on about a place that's not twenty minutes' fast drive from here, signposted clear as the City of London!"

Suddenly Harvey's unwashed features paled visibly. "You mean you've actually seen this place?" he whispered. "And you drove past...High House?"

"Damn right!" George answered, abruptly feeling as though things were all unreal, a very vivid but meaningless daydream. Harvey lifted a flap in the counter and waddled through to George's side. He was a very big man, George suddenly noticed, and the color had come back to his face with a vengeance. There was a red, angry tinge to the man's sallow features now; moreover, the cafeteria was quite empty of other souls, all bar the two of them.

"Now look here—" George blurted, as Harvey began to maneuver him into a corner.

"I shouldn't 'av mentioned 'is money, should I?" the fat man cut him off, his piggy eyes fastening upon those of his patently intended victim, making his question more a statement than a question proper.

"See," he continued, "I'd 'ad a couple of pints earlier, or I wouldn't 'ave let it drop about 'is predicament. 'E's been right good to me, Mr. Kent 'as. 'Elped me set this place up proper, 'e did—an' I don't cotton to the idea of some flyboy tryin' to—"

Again his arm shot out and he grabbed Benson's throat this time, trapping him in the dim corner. "So you've been down the road to Middle Hamborough, 'ave you?—And you've seen High House, eh? Well, let me tell you, I've been looking for that place close on six years, me an' ol' Kent, an' not so much as a peep!

"Now I knows 'e's a bit of a nut, but I *like* 'im an' we gets on fine. Stays 'ere, cheap like, 'e does, an' we do a bit of motorin' in 'is ol' car—lookin' for those places you say you've seen, y'know? But we never finds 'em, an' we never will, 'cos they're not there, see? Kent bein' a decent gent, I 'umors 'im an' things is OK. But I'm no crook, if you see what I mean, though I'm not so sure I can say the same for everybody!"

He peered pointedly at George, releasing the pressure on his windpipe enough for him to croak: "I tell you I have seen High House, or at least, I saw a place of that name and answering the description I heard from Kent. And I have been on the road to—"

"What's that about High House?" The question was a hoarse, quavering whisper—hesitant, and yet filled with excited expectancy. Hearing that whisper, Harvey immediately released his grip on Benson's neck and turned to move over quickly to the thin, gray-haired, middle-aged man who had appeared out of a back room behind the service counter.

"Don't get yourself all upset, Mr. Kent," Harvey protested, holding up his hands solicitously. "It's just some bloke tryin' to pull a fast one, an'—"

"But I heard him say—" Kent's eyes were wide, staring past the fat proprietor straight at Benson where he stood, still shaken, in the corner.

George found his voice again. "I said I'd seen High House, on the road to Middle Hamborough—and I did see it." He shook himself, straightening his tie and shrugging his disarranged jacket back into position. "But I didn't come back in here to get involved with a couple of nuts. And I don't think much of your joke."

George turned away and made for the door; then, remembering his previous trouble, he turned back to face Harvey. "Do you have a map of the area by any chance? I've been in Germany for a long time and seem to be out of touch over here. I can't seem to find my way about anymore."

For a moment Kent continued to stare very hard at the speaker; then he turned to Harvey. "He—he got lost! And he says he's seen High House…! I've got to believe him. I daren't miss the chance that—"

Almost sure by now that he was the victim of some cockeyed leg-pull (and yet still experiencing niggling little subconscious doubts), George Benson shrugged. "OK. No map," he grumbled. "Well, goodnight, boys. Maybe I'll drop in again sometime—like next visiting day!"

"No, wait!" the thin man cried. "Do you think that you can find…that you can find High House again?" His voice went back to a whisper on the last half dozen words.

"Sure, I can find it again," George told him, nodding his head. "But it's well out of my way."

"I'll make it worth your trouble," Kent quickly answered, his voice rising rapidly in what sounded to George like a bad case of barely suppressed hysteria. "I'll make it very worthwhile indeed!"

George was not the man to pass up a good thing. "My car's outside," he said. "Do you want to ride with me, or will you follow in your own car?"

"I'll ride with you. My hands are shaking so badly that I—"

"I'm coming with you," Harvey suddenly grunted, taking off his greasy apron.

"No, no, my friend," Kent turned to him. "If we don't find High House, I'll be back. Until then, and just in case we do find it, this is for all you've done." His hand was still shaking as he took out a checkbook and quickly, nervously, scribbled. He passed the check to Harvey and George managed to get a good look at it. His eyes went wide when he saw the amount it was made out for. Five hundred pounds!

"Now look 'ere, Mr. Kent," Harvey blustered. "I don't like the looks of this bloke. I reckon—"

"I understand your concern," the older man told him, "but I'm sure Mr.—?" he turned to George.

"Er, Smith," George told him, unwilling to reveal his real name. This could still be some crazy joke, but if so, it would be on some bloke called "Smith," and not on George Benson!

"I'm sure that Mr. Smith is legitimate. And in any case I daren't miss the chance to get...to get back home." He was eager now to be on his way. "Are you ready, Mr. Smith?"

"Just as soon as you say," George told him. "The sooner the better."

They walked out into the night, to George's car, leaving fat greasy Harvey worriedly squeezing his hands in the doorway to his all-nighter. Suddenly the night air seemed inordinately cold, and as George opened the passenger door to let Kent get in, he shivered. He walked round the. car, climbed into the driver's seat and slammed the door.

As George started up the motor, Kent spoke up from where he crouched against the opposite door, a huddled shape in the dark interior of the car. "Are you sure that—that—"

"Look," George answered, the utter craziness of the whole business abruptly dawning on him, souring his voice, "if this is some sort of nutty joke...." He let the threat hang, then snapped, "Of course I can find it again! High House, you're talking about?"

"Yes, yes. High House. The home I built for the woman who lives there, waiting for me."

"For fifteen years?" George allowed himself to indulge in the other's fantasy.

"She would wait until time froze!" Kent leaned over to spit the words in George's ear. "And in any case, I have a theory."

Yeah! George thought to himself. *Me, too!* Out loud, he said, "A theory?"

"Yes. I think—I hope—it's possible that time itself is frozen at the moment of the fracture. If I can get back, it may all be unchanged. I may even regain my lost years!"

"A parallel dimension, eh?" George said, feeling strangely nervous.

"Right," his passenger nodded emphatically. "That's the way I see it."

Humoring him, George asked, "What's it like, this other world of yours?"

"Why, it's just like this world—except that there's a village called Middle Hamborough, and a house on a hill, and a building firm called Milton, Jones & Kent. There are probably other differences, too, but I haven't found any yet to concern me. Do you know the theory of parallel worlds?"

"I've read some science fiction," George guardedly answered. "Some of these other dimensions, or whatever they're supposed to be, are just like this world. Maybe a few odd differences, like you say. Others are different, completely different. Horrible and alien—stuff like that." He suddenly felt stupid. "That's what I've read, anyway. Load of rubbish!"

"Rubbish?" Kent grunted, stirring in his seat. "I wish it were. But, anyway, you've got the right idea. Why are you stopping?"

"See that sign?" George said, pointing through the windscreen to where the headlights lit up a village sign-post. "Meadington, just a few miles down the road. We're through Meadington in about five minutes. Then we turn left where it's signposted to Middle Hamborough. Another five minutes after that and we're at High House. You said it would be worth my while?"

Now comes the crunch, George told himself. *This is where the idiot bursts out laughing—and that's when I brain him.*

But Kent didn't laugh. Instead he got out his checkbook, and George switched on the interior light to watch him write a note for….

George's eyes bulged as he saw the numbers go down on the crisp paper. First a one, followed by three zeros! One thousand pounds! "This won't bounce?" he asked suspiciously, his hand trembling as he reached for the check.

"It won't bounce," said Kent, folding the note and tucking it into his pocket. "Fortunately, my money was good for this world, too. You get it when we get to High House."

"You have a deal," George told him, putting the car in gear. They drove through slumbering Meadington, its roofs and hedges silvered in a moonlight that shone through the promise of a mist. Leaving the village behind; the car sped along the country road, but after a few minutes George pulled into the curb and stopped. His passenger had slumped down in his seat. "Are you OK?" George asked.

"There's no turnoff," Kent sobbed. "We should have passed it before now. I've driven down this road a thousand, five thousand times in the last fifteen years, and tonight it's just the same as always. There's no turnoff, no signpost to Middle Hamborough!"

"Yeah." George chewed his lip, unwilling to accept defeat so easily. "We must have missed it. It wasn't this far out of Meadington last time." He turned the big car about, driving on to the grass verge to do so, then headed back towards Meadington.

George was angry now and more than a little puzzled. He'd been watching for that signpost as keenly as his passenger. How the hell could they have missed it? No matter, this time he'd drive dead slow. He knew the road was there, for he'd been down it and back once already tonight.

Sure enough, with the first of Meadington's roofs glimmering silver in the near distance, a dilapidated signpost suddenly showed up in the beam of the car's lights. It pointed across the tarmac to where the surface of a second road ribboned away into the milky moonlight; a sign whose legend, though grimy, was nevertheless amply legible: MIDDLE HAMBOROUGH.

And quite as suddenly George Benson's passenger was sitting bolt upright in his seat, his whole body visibly trembling while his eyes stood out like organ stops, staring madly at the signpost. "Middle Hamborough!" he cried, his voice pitched so high it almost broke. And again: "Middle Hamborough, Middle Hamborough!"

"Sure," said George, an unnatural chill racing up his spine. "I told you I could find it!" And to himself he added, *But I'm damned if I know how we missed it the first time!*

He turned on to the new road, noticing the second signpost at his right as he did so. That was the one they'd missed. Perhaps it had been in the shadows; but in any case, what odds? They were on the right road now.

Kent's trembling had stopped, and his voice was quite steady when he said, "You really don't know how much I owe you, Mr. Smith. You shall have your check, of course, but if it were for a million pounds it wouldn't really be enough." His face was dark in the car's interior, and his silhouette looked different somehow.

George said, "You realize that fat Harvey's been having you on all this time, don't you?" His voice became quite gentle as he added: "You know, you really ought to see someone about it—about all…this, I mean. People can take advantage of you. Harvey could have brought you here any time he wanted."

Suddenly Kent laughed, a young laugh that had more than a trace of weary hysteria in it. "Oh, you don't know the half of it, do you, Mr. Smith? Can't you get it through your head that I'm not mad and no one is trying to make a fool of you? This is all real. My story is the truth. I was lost in an alien dimension, in your world, but now I'm finally back in my own. You may believe me, Mr. Smith, that you have earned your thousand pounds!"

George was almost convinced. Certainly Kent seemed sincere enough. "Well, OK—whatever you say. But I'll tell you something, Mr. Kent. If that check of yours bounces when I try to cash it tomorrow, I'll be back, and you better believe I'll find High House again!"

The silhouette turned in its seat in an attitude of concern. "Do me a favor, will you, Mr. Smith? If—just *if*, you understand—if you can't find the road back to Meadington, don't hesitate to—"

George cut him off with a short bark of a laugh. "You must be joking! I'll find it, all right." His voice went hard again. "And I'll find you, too, if—"

But he paused as, at the top of the next low hill, the headlights illuminated a house standing above the road at the end of a winding drive. George's passenger grabbed his elbow in terrific excitement. "High House!" Kent cried, his voice wild and exultant. "High House! You've done it!"

George grunted in answer, revving the car down into the valley and up the hill to pull in to a halt outside the wrought-iron gates. He reached across to catch hold of his passenger's coat as Kent tried to scramble from the car. "Kent!"

"Oh, yes, your check," answered the young man, turning to smile excitedly at George in the yellow light from the little lamp on the gate....

George's jaw dropped. Oh, this was Kent, all right. Little doubt about that. Same features, same suit, same trembling hand that reached into a pocket to bring out the folded check and place it in George's suddenly clammy hand. But it was a hand that trembled now in excitement and not frustrated but undying hope—and it was a Kent *fifteen* years younger!

One thousand pounds, and at last George knew that he had indeed earned it!

Kent turned and threw open the gates, racing up the drive like a wild man. In the house, lights were starting to go on. George fingered his check unbelievingly and ran his tongue over dry lips. His mind seemed to have frozen over, so that only one phrase kept repeating in his brain. It was something Kent had said: "If you can't find the road back to—"

He gunned the motor, spinning the car wildly round in a spray of gravel chips. Up on the hill at the top of the drive, Kent was vaulting the fence, and a figure in white was waiting in the garden for him, open arms held wide. George tore his eyes away from them and roared down the hill. For the second time that night he headed for the Meadington road.

The check lay on the empty passenger seat now where he'd dropped it, and money was quite the last thing in George's mind as he drove his car in an unreasoning panic, leaping the low hills like some demon hurdler as he tried to make it back to the main road before—before what? A hideous doubt was blossoming in his mind, growing like some evil genie from a bottle and taking on a horrible form.

All those stories about queer dislocations of space and time—the signpost for Middle Hamborough that was, then wasn't, then was again—and of course Kent's story, and his...rejuvenation?

"I will be very glad," George told himself out loud, "when I reach that junction just outside Meadington!" For one thing, he could have sworn that it wasn't this much of a drive. He should surely have been there by now. Ah, yes, this would be it coming up now, just round this slight bend....

No junction!

The road stretched straight on ahead, narrow and suddenly ominous in the sweeping beam of his lights. All right, so the junction was a little further than he'd reckoned. George put his foot down even harder to send the big car racing along the narrow road. The miles flew by without a single signpost or junction, and a ground mist came in that forced George to slow down. He would have done so anyway, for now the road seemed to be exerting a strange pull on his car. The big motor felt as if it were slowing down! George's heart almost jumped into his mouth. There couldn't be anything wrong with the car, could there?

Braking to a halt and switching off the car's engine and lights, George climbed out of the driver's seat. He breathed the damp night air. On unpleasantly rubbery legs he walked round to the front of the car and lifted the hood. An inspection light came on and he cast a quick, practiced glance over the motor. No, he'd worked in a garage for many years and he knew a good motor when he saw one. Nothing wrong with the car, so—

As he straightened up, George felt an unaccustomed suction on his shoes and glanced down at the road. The surface was rubbery, formed of a sort of tough sponge. A worried frown crossed George's face as he bent to feel that peculiar surface. He'd never seen a road surfaced with stuff like that before!

It was as he straightened up again that he heard the tinkling, like the sound of tiny bells from somewhere off the road. Yes, there, set back from the road, he could make out a row of low squat houses, like great mushrooms partly obscured by the mist that swirled now in strange currents. The tinkling came from the houses.

The outskirts of a village? George wondered. Well, at least he'd be able to get directions. He stepped off the road on to turf and made for the houses, only slowing down when he saw how featureless and alike they all looked. The queer tinkling went on, sounding like the gentle noises that the hangings on a Christmas tree make in a draught. Other than that there were only the billowing mist and the darkness.

Reaching the first house, stepping very slowly now, George came up close to the wall and stared at it. It was gray, completely featureless. All the houses looked alike. They were indeed like enormous mushrooms. No windows. Overhanging roofs. Flaps of sorts that might just be doors, or there again—

The tinkling had stopped. Very carefully George reached out and touched the wall in front of him. It felt warm…and it crept beneath his fingers!

Deliberately and slowly George turned about and forced one foot out in front of the other. Then he took a second step. He fought the urge to look back over his shoulder until, halfway to the mist-wreathed car, he heard an odd plopping sound behind him. It was like the *ploop* you get throwing a handful of mud into a pond. He froze with his back still turned to the houses.

Quite suddenly he felt sure that his ears were enlarging, stretching back and up to form saucer-like receivers on top of his head. Everything he had went into those ears, and all of it was trying to tune in to what was going on behind him. He didn't turn, but simply stood still; and again there was only the utter silence, loud in his strangely sensitized ears. He forced his dead feet to take a few more paces forward—and sure enough the sound came again, repeating this time: *ploop, ploop, ploop!*

George slowly pivoted on his heel as muscles he never knew he had began to jump in his face. The noises, each *ploop* sounding closer than the last, stopped immediately. His legs felt like twin columns of jelly, but he somehow completed his turn. He stumbled spastically then, arms flailing to keep himself from falling. The nearest house, or cottage, or whatever, was right there behind him, within arm's reach.

Suddenly George's heart, which he was sure had stopped for ever, became audible again inside him, banging away in his chest like a trip-hammer. All in one movement he turned and bounded for the car, wondering why with each leap he should stay so long in the air, knowing that in fact his body was moving like greased lightning while his mind (in an even greater hurry, one his body couldn't even attempt to match) thought he was in reverse!

Not bothering, not *daring* to look back again, he almost wrenched the car door from its hinges as he threw himself into the driving seat. Then, in an instant that lasted several centuries, his hand was on the ignition key and the engine was roaring. As he spun the car about in a squeal of tortured tires and accelerated up the rubbery road, he looked in his rearview mirror—and immediately wished he hadn't!

The "houses" were all *ploop*ing down the road after him—like great greedy frogs—and their "doors" were wide open!

George nearly went off the road then, wrenching at the wheel with clammy hands as he fought to control his careening car on the peculiar surface. A million monstrous thoughts raced through his head as he climbed up through the gears. For of course he knew now for certain that he was trapped in an alien dimension, that the space-time elastic had snapped back into place behind him, stranding him here. Wherever "here" was!

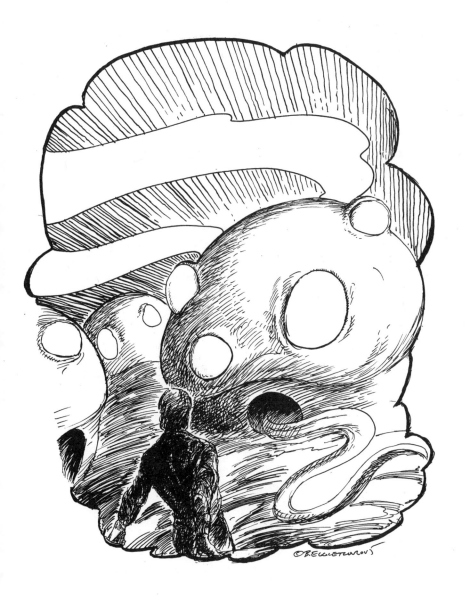

It was only several miles later that he thought to slow down, and only then after passing a junction on the right and a signpost saying: MIDDLE HAMBOROUGH 5 MILES. His heart gave a wild leap as he skidded to a halt on a once more perfectly normal tarmac road. Why, that sign meant that just half a mile up the road in front he'd find Meadington, and beyond Meadington...Bankhead and the Ml!...Except that Meadington wasn't there.... Instead, the mist came up again and, worse, the road went rubbery. And no sign of Meadington. When he saw a row of mushroom "houses" standing back from the road, George did an immediate, violent about-turn, rocking the car dangerously on the rubbery road. Trouble with this weird surface was that it gave too much damn traction.

Amazing that he could still think such mundane thoughts in a situation like this. And yet, through all of this protracted nightmare, a ray of hope still shone. The road to Middle Hamborough!

Back there, down that road, there was a house on a hill and beyond that a real, if slightly different, world. A world where at least two of the inhabitants owed him a break. From what Kent had told him, it seemed to George that the other world wasn't much different from his own. He could make a go of things there. He gunned his motor back down the road and out of the mist, back on to a decent tarmac surface and into normally dark night, turning left at the leaning signpost on to the now familiar road to Middle Hamborough.

Or was it familiar?

The hedges bordering the road were different somehow, taller, hiding the fields beyond them from the car's probing headlights, and the road seemed narrower than George remembered it. But that must be his imagination acting up after the terrific shocks of the last ten or twenty minutes; it had to be, for this was the road to Middle Hamborough.

Then, cresting the next hill, suddenly George felt that hellish drag on his tires, and his headlights began to do battle with a thickening, swirling mist. At the same time he saw the house atop the next hill, the house set back off the road at the head of a long winding drive. High House!

There were no lights on in the place now, but it was George's refuge none the less. Hadn't Kent told him to come back here if he couldn't find his way back to Meadington? George gave a whoop of relief as he swept down into the shallow valley and up the hill towards the wrought-iron roadside gates. They were still open, as Kent had left them; and as he slowed down fractionally, George swung the wheel to the left, turning his car in through the gates. They weren't quite open all the way, though, so that the front of the car slammed them back on their hinges.

Up the drive the front lights of the house instantly came on; two of them glowed yellow as though shutters had been quickly opened—or lids lifted! George had no time to note anything else—except perhaps that the drive was very white, not the white of gravel but more of leprous flesh— for at that point the car simply stopped as if it had run head-on into a brick wall! George wasn't belted in. He rose up over the steering wheel and crashed through the windscreen, automatically turning his shoulder to the glass.

He hit the drive in a shower of glass fragments, screaming and expecting the impact to hurt. It didn't, and then George knew why the car had stopped like that: the drive was as soft and sticky as hot toffee. And it wasn't a drive!

Behind George the wide fleshy ribbon tasted the car and, rising up, flicked it easily to one side. Then it tasted George. He had time to scream, barely, and time for one more quite mundane thought—that this wasn't where Kent lived—before that great white chameleon tongue slithered him up the hill to the house, whose entire front below the yellow windows opened up to receive him.

Shortly thereafter the lights went slowly out again, as if someone had lowered shutters, or as if lids had fallen....

The Man Who
Saw No Spiders

In mid-1977 (yes, I was still in the Army), I wrote "The Man Who Saw No Spiders." An arachnophobe, me? Naaah! But I know a lot of people are, and I don't confine my fiction to things that scare just me; I enjoy giving other people the shudders, too. I mean, that's what it's all about, right? Entertainment? No? Ah, well, to each his own.

Anyway, two years later W. Paul Ganley used the story in his award-winning small press magazine *Weirdbook 13*... and that's about all I can say about it. But if *you* haven't seen any spiders just lately, or if you should find that you don't even want to *think* about them—

—Er, what was I saying?

"HE WHAT?" ASKED BLEAKER, Conway's neighbor, incredulously.

Conway smiled at his friend's astounded expression, then repeated himself, adding: "It's quite genuine, I assure you, Jerry. He won't admit of spiders. They don't exist for him."

"Then of course he's a madman," Bleaker shrugged. "I mean, it's like someone saying he doesn't believe in mushrooms...isn't it?"

"Not at all," Conway answered. "The man who says he doesn't believe in mushrooms at least admits of their theory—by the very act of naming them—if you see what I mean?"

"Frankly, no," Bleaker shook his head, reaching for his drink. He lived only a short walk away from Conway, along a beautifully wooded path, set back half a mile from the main road that wound out from the nearby town and over the hills northward. The area was lonely but lovely and a handful of well-to-do families had their homes on the edge of the woods that stretched away to the hills. Bleaker and Conway had built comparatively close together, hence they were "neighbors," even though their houses stood almost a quarter-mile apart.

"OK, Jerry, look at it this way," Conway persisted. "If I say I don't believe in God, then there's not a great deal you can do to convince me that God does indeed exist, is there? No I'm not trying to be offensive, I assure you. I could just as easily have made it Father Christmas or Easter Bunny. However, while I don't admit of a God, I can readily enough understand others who do believe. I know what they are on about; I understand the theory of it."

"Yes, but—" Bleaker began, wishing that the girls would come on out of Conway's kitchen and get him off his psychiatric hobbyhorse.

"—But suppose I refuse to accept something as tangible as a good old-fashioned English mushroom. What then?"

"Why, then I bring you one, Paul. I let you touch it, smell it, eat the bloody thing! I show you the word in an encyclopedia with a picture of the real thing alongside. I get out a dictionary and spell it out for you: m-u-s-h-r-o-o-m...! I take you into town, the market on a Friday, where I buy you a pound of them. You can't escape them, they're there. Mushrooms *are*—you have to accept them." He sat back, smiling at his own cleverness.

"Good!" said Conway, successful psychiatrist written all over his face. "Now then, assume that when you bring me the mushroom I ignore it. Assume that my senses won't, *can't* recognize it. Assume that when I look at your dictionary I see 'mush' above and 'mushiness' below, but no 'mushroom' in between. That I don't even hear you when you say the word 'mushroom.' That I wonder why you're making funny faces when you spell the word out for me. What then?"

"Then you're a nut, pure and simple."

"Oh? And suppose that in every other instance I am a perfectly normal human being. An upstanding member of the community. A happily married man with no problems worth mentioning. In short, assume that in every way save one it's clearly demonstrable that I am *not* a nut. How about that?"

Bleaker frowned. "Hmm.... Could you possibly have some new, weird, exotic disease? Shall we call it, say, 'fungitis'? Even then, though, it has to be a disease of the mind. However harmless you are, you still have to be a nut."

Conway looked disappointed. "Yes, well the man we're talking about is not a nut. He's Thomas Waterford, gamekeeper for Lord Daventry at The Lodge. And with him it's not mushrooms but spiders. He doesn't believe in them, can't see them, he might as well never have heard of them. And from what I've seen of him, he'll never hear of them again."

"He's a nut," Bleaker insisted, without emphasis.

"He's as sane as you or I," Conway denied. "I've used every trick in the psychiatric book to test his sanity and I'm certain of it."

"So what caused it then?" Bleaker demanded to know. "Has he always been this way?"

"Ah! Good question. No, he hasn't always been this way; I was lucky to get onto him so quickly. It started a week ago yesterday, on a Saturday morning. Rather it started on the Friday, when his wife asked him to clean all of the cobwebs and spiders out of the cellar of the gatehouse where they live. She hates spiders, you see. Yes, that was on the Friday. He told her he was busy, said that Lord Daventry was worried about poachers and he'd be out in the woods for most of the night, but that he'd clean out the spiders in the morning. He *believed* in spiders then, you see? But when she reminded him on the Saturday he ignored her. And when she took him down into the cellar to see how badly infested the place was, he—"

"He couldn't see the spiders?"

"Right! At first she thought he was kidding her on, but later she started to worry about it. On Monday she told Lord Daventry about it and he had a go at Old Thomas. Then he contacted me. It seemed such an interesting case that I took it on gratis, as a favor. I drove over the hills to The Lodge that same afternoon...." He paused.

Interested despite himself, Bleaker prompted him: "And?"

"Jerry, it's like nothing I ever dealt with before. For the last five or six days spiders have had no place whatsoever in Thomas Waterford's life. Here, listen to this tape. I recorded it on Wednesday morning, five days after the thing began." He went over to his tape recorder and pressed a button, listening as snatches of speeded-up conversation babbled forth until he found the spot he was looking for. A second button slowed the tape down and the recorded conversation became audible:

"*Well, we really don't seem to be getting anywhere, do we, Thomas?*"

"*P'raps we would, sir, if I knew what you was after. I've plenty of work on at The Lodge, and—*"

"*But Lord Daventry said you'd be only too happy to help me out, Thomas.*"

"*'Course, sir, but we don't seem to be doing much really, do we? I mean— wot am I 'ere for?*"

"*Spiders, Thomas!*"

(Silence)

"*Why are you afraid of them?*"

"*Afraid of wot, sir?*"

"*Creepy-crawlies.*"

"*Wot, bugs and beetles and flies, sir? I hain't scared of 'em, sir! Wotever made you think that?*"

"*No, I meant spiders, Thomas, Hairy-legged web-spinners!*"

"*I mean, I sees bugs every day in the woods, I do, and—*"

"*And birds?*"

"*Lots of 'em.*"

"*And trees?*"

"*'Ere, you're' aving me on!*"

"*And—spiders?*"

"*'Course I sees trees! The 'ole bleedin' forest's full of 'em!*"

Conway speeded the tape up at this point, and while it crackled and blustered on he said to Bleaker, "Listen to this next bit. This was the next day, Thursday. I had some rough drawings for Thomas to look at...."

He slowed the tape down and after a few seconds Bleaker heard the following:

"*Just have a look at this, Thomas, will you? What do you reckon that is?*"

"*Bird, sir. Thrush, I'd say, but not a very good drawing.*"

"*And this one?*"

"*An eft. Newt, you'd call it, but I've always called 'em efts.*"

"*And this?*"

"*A tree, probably a hoak—but wot's the point of all—*"

"*And—this?*"

"*Blank, sir. A blank piece of paper!*"

(Pause, then a cough from Conway.)

"*And how about, er, this?*"

"*A bleedin' happle, sir!*"

"*Yes, but what's on the apple?*"

"*Eh? Why, a stalk, and a leaf.*"

"*And?...What's this thing here, staring at you?*"

"*'Ere! You're 'aving me on again, hain't you? There's nothin' there 'cept your finger, sir!...*"

Conway switched the tape recorder off. He looked at Bleaker and said, "Both the 'blank' and the thing on the apple were—"

"Spiders?"

Conway nodded.

At that point the women came in from the kitchen carrying plated salads. "Spiders!" exclaimed Dorothy, Conway's wife, in disgust. She turned to Bleaker. "Don't tell me he's going on about old Tom Waterford again? I've had to listen to nothing else for a week!"

"But this sounds *so* interesting," said Bleaker's wife, Andrea. "What's it all about? One of your cases, Paul?"

Dorothy held up her hand and took charge of the situation before it could get out of hand. "No you don't, Paul, not tonight. You've got Jerry here bored stiff. And anyway, I've told you what the answer is."

"Oh?" Bleaker looked at her. "What do you reckon then, Dorothy?"

She held up a finger and shushed them, looking very serious. "Flying saucers!" she said.

They all laughed.

"Oh, it's not so funny," she cautioned, unable to avoid giggling, despite her semi-serious expression. "It was just before Old Tom went funny that the light was seen over the hills."

"A light?" Andrea repeated, completely out of her depth.

"Yes, a queer light, over the hills near Lord Daventry's place," Dorothy said. "Myself, I reckon the Martians got Old Tom!" And again they all laughed; but Dorothy laughed loudest for she'd succeeded in changing the subject, which was all she had wanted to do….

The "lights" were seen again much later that same night, this time from the other side of the hills. Lord Daventry, sitting in his study, caught the bluish flash out of the corner of his eye as he sat studying some papers. Looking out of his window, away over the hills he saw a beam of light like a solid bar striking from heaven to the earth. It lasted for just a second, then was gone, but it reminded him of similar lights he had seen over a week ago. That had been about the time that Old Tom started his queer business.

Thinking about his gamekeeper made the peer suddenly wonder how Conway was getting on with the case. Lord Daventry knew that the psychiatrist had spent a fair amount of time with Thomas.

Well, Conway usually worked late, didn't he? There was no reason why he shouldn't call the man up and find out how things stood. They were, after all, old friends of sorts. Perhaps he'd also ask if Conway had seen the light. He thought about it for a few minutes more, then picked up his telephone and dialed Conway's number.

He heard the answering *brrp, brrp, brrp,* from the other end, then the distant telephone was lifted from its cradle in Conway's study. "Conway?" said the Lord. "I hope I've not got you out of bed?"

"Not at all," Conway's voice came back, promptly and clearly. "I was doing a bit of work. Had a drink with some friends earlier but they're long gone. Dorothy's in bed."

"Good. I just wondered if you'd seen that peculiar light? I saw it a minute or so ago from my window. Seemed to shine down pretty close to your place. Funny sort of thing...."

Conway didn't answer. He was staring out of his own window. Out there, just beyond the dense copse at the foot of the garden, emitting a pul-sing sort of auroral radiance whose like he had never in his life seen before, the bluish dome of an alien vessel showed like an obscene blister against the background of nighted hills. Closer to the house, looking at Conway where he stood star-ing out of the window, something loomed on stilt-like legs—something huge, hairy and hideously ugly beyond nightmare—something much more monstrously alien than the spacecraft which had brought it here.

It was, of sorts, a spider—but already Conway was beginning to forget that there were such things.

The bushes at the side of the house, from which even now a smaller spider emerged, swaying almost mechanically into view; the garden and copse and blister of strange light beyond; the dark backdrop of hills and roof of star-strewn skies: all of these things were peripheral in Conway's awareness, as the frame of a picture seen close-up is peripheral in the eye of the viewer. His concentration, to the contrary, was *centered* on the spi-der, on its eyes.

At the other end of the wire, Lord Daventry waited patiently for an answer. After a little while, wondering at the delay, he asked: "Paul? Are you still there?"

Conway, staring into the vast, crimson, hooded orbs of the thing's eyes where they glared at him hypnotically from the garden, shook his head as if to clear away some mental smog. He finally answered:

"Yes, I'm here. Could you repeat what you said just then? I didn't catch it the first time."

"I said did you see the strange light?"

"No, I saw no light." Conway made no attempt to enlarge upon the subject.

Believing Conway must be tired, the peer decided to keep the conver-sation short. "Ah...." he cleared his throat. "Look, sorry to be a nuisance, Paul, but I was wondering about Old Thomas...." He paused.

Conway made no comment.

"Old Thomas," repeated the peer more loudly, becoming frustrated. "Thomas and his spiders!" His voice came sharp and clear, if a little tinny, from Conway's telephone.

Conway grunted impatiently and frowned. He jiggled the telephone, blew into the earpiece, and said: "Look, I'm sorry, sir. Terrible line tonight. Can't hear a thing you're saying. Can I ring you back in the morning?" And with that he replaced the receiver.

He was dimly, hazily aware, while he performed these casual, automatic tasks, that the smaller of the two creatures outside bore in its mandibles the body of Andrea Bleaker—that as its mouth worked avidly at her middle, the uppermost of its three globular semi-opaque abdomen-sacks was turning a dull red—but this also was peripheral knowledge. Not once did his attention waver from the eyes of the larger creature. He couldn't divert his attention if he tried.

That night thirty thousand backup vessels beamed in, an entire taskforce, most of them far bigger than the half-dozen or so scout craft already in situ. In the morning Conway made his telephone call, as he had promised, to Lord Daventry, but there was no answer. At midnight a craft had landed in the peer's garden and its pilot had been hungry.

By midday there were still one or two pockets of uninitiated people in isolated places—the odd Eskimo family or settlement, a reclusive order of Tibetan monks, the crew of a marine survey vessel just north of the southern pack ice—all of whom still believed in spiders, but not many. As for the invaders: there were not especially worried about finding these as yet unbranded mavericks. That could wait.

Right now there was the herding to think about, and then the giant factory ships would have to be brought in....

Deja Viewer

Now we fast forward almost quarter of a century to 2002. I was trying to give myself a break, get away from writing novels for a while, which I seemed to have been doing almost nonstop since retiring (from the Army in December 1980). Now, I'm the kind of fellow who often has odd or peculiar thoughts (what do you mean, you would never have guessed!?) and it had recently occurred to me that when I look in a mirror I don't see myself as I *am* but as I *was* the tiniest fraction of a second ago… because light isn't an instantaneous medium. In fact there are no instantaneous media—except, or so we're informed—in "quantum entanglement." (Okay, so you knew that.) Anyway, that is the thought which led me to this next story, and to say anything else about it, except where it first appeared, in a limited edition, small press British publication called *Maelstrom Vol. 1,* Calvin House 2004, would simply mean giving it away.

(And as for giving it away, well the title doesn't help too much, either!)

YES IT'S POSSIBLE. And yes, I'm pretty sure they'll do it one day, even if I'm no longer in the program. Which I won't be, not the way I am now. But best to begin at the beginning, back when I was eight or nine years old.

I had wanted to be an astronaut…*huh!* Bad timing. Just when all of that was winding down. And here we are in 2044 and it never did wind up again, not all the way. Oh, there've been more Mars probes, and gas-giant moon probes, but all automated, computer driven, and no astronauts worth the mention. We still have the manned, Lego-like, Earth-orbiting international space-station twirling and twinkling away up there, and the

Moonbase that no one's been back to for seven years since its dome was popped by a pea-sized Leonid meteorite, but that's it, that's your lot.

No great future in astronautics, obviously.

But with my grades I could at least theorize on space, the universe and like that, even if I wasn't going to go out there. And with my aptitude for physics—of the more truly physical variety as opposed to, or hand in hand with, the theoretical—I certainly wasn't going to miss out on a job in some research laboratory; just about any research facility, for that matter. But the dreams (in fact they were nightmares) came a long time before that, when I was eight or nine years old….

They were sort of vague at first.

I remember my father comforting me, sitting on my bed with his arm around me, holding me tight. "What was all that about?" he asked me, with a frown on a face that mine was the image of except for all the lines, that face which on waking I imagined had solidified right out of my nightmare, causing me to shrink back from him. "What was it, Davy? Some kind of bad dream?"

And I remember telling him, "It was a face—I think it was your face, Dad—but the mouth was all twisted up and hurting, and the face was all blurred. You were shouting at me, I think. Telling me not to do it." And I sat there shivering.

"I was telling you not to do it? Hey, what's all this, son? Are you feeling guilty about something?"

Guilty? Me? But have you ever known a nine-year-old boy who *didn't* feel guilty about something or other? Like his curiosity about girls and their differences? Or the stolen cigarette that made him sick behind the garden shed last Thursday? Or the ten-dollar bill he found in the road and didn't tell the neighborhood cop about? Or the sparrow he killed with his BB gun before putting the weapon in its box and locking it, and shoving it to the back of a shelf where he couldn't any longer see it; out of sight, out of mind sort of thing? Of course I felt guilty. But that's not what the dream had been about. And so:

"No," I told him, still shivering in his arms. "It was just a dream—a bad dream, that's all—but it's gone now." Which was true enough at the time, except I didn't know then that it hadn't gone very far. Or not far enough….

It happened a good many times after that, too many times, while I was still a kid; but on every occasion it was dark and vague, just like the first time, like a bad memory that keeps floating to the surface but never enough that you recognize its origin or what it's about. Guilt? Conscience? No. I don't think so. I mean, I had never done anything *that* bad, had I? Apart from the usual troubles that kids get into my childhood had been pretty much idyllic. I had loved my Ma and Da, and in return had been much loved.

Yet I must have been to blame for something. The dream, my nightmare, must surely be *something* out of my past, some badly scarred bit of mental baggage or other. Or so I supposed, as I quickly came to dread it without quite knowing why. For let's face it: it wasn't that much of a nightmare, now was it? What, a dark blurred face and an obscure warning?

That was all it was, yes. Yet every time it came I would wake up in my clammy, tumbled bed, with those anxious, urgent, distant but *insistent* demands echoing over and over in my head even as they receded:

"Don't do it! Don't do it! Don't make it happen! For God' sake, don't...do...it!"

There were periods, weeks and months at a time, when I slept deep and peacefully and my dreams were nothing much out of the ordinary. And at times like that I tended to forget about the vague visage and its meaningless warning. Or rather I *tried* to forget it, tried hard to convince myself that whatever it had been, whatever the dream had meant, it was done with now and no longer meant anything.

I tried to put it to the back of my mind, tried to cage it there; a tactic that seemed to work, at least at first. But any reprieve I might have gained was always temporary—it wouldn't *stay* caged. Eventually, invariably, it would regroup, refashion itself, and return out of limbo to start tormenting me all over again. And again there would be times when it totally dominated the dark hours, as regular and recurrent as the night itself.

Yet somehow I learned to live with it. Oh, I worried about it—and worried more than a little about the state of my mind—of course I did, who wouldn't? But since it obviously wasn't going to go away...well, as that old saw has it, "familiarity breeds contempt." But in fact it wasn't so much contempt as an awareness that there was nothing I could do about it,

In my early teens, following a year long hiatus, the nightmare returned in a new, far more disturbing format. Where before its main focus had centered upon a blurred, twisted, frustratingly familiar face, now any sense of familiarity—of recognition, however remote—was absent, replaced by something completely unknown and utterly terrifying.

It happened like this:

Having earned a course of advanced education as a reward for my exceptional grades in Jr. High, I was attending a local college and sleeping at home. On the night the dream returned, taking on this more definite, truly horrific form, my parents were visiting with friends and didn't hear my shouting…or more properly my screaming. I'm not ashamed to admit it: this time I woke up screaming for my life, screaming my lungs out!

In the dream:

At first there was only the darkness and a certain uneasy awareness; I had felt this before, and so knew what was coming. Then the darkness swirled, like smoke made luminous in the beam of a movie projector. And there in the gloom, out of this weird ectoplasm, the face gradually firmed up, coalescing into a more solid projection. But it wasn't the usual face, or at least it didn't seem to be. And:

"*Don't!*" That ethereal warning, even before the thing had fully developed. "*Don't do it! For God's sake, don't!*"

I wanted to answer—to ask what it was I mustn't do—but my mouth was dry, made clammy with sleep and fear. And all the time this foggy outline putting on flesh…or losing it? For abruptly, as suddenly and shockingly as that, the face was full-formed. But it wasn't nearly a full face! And:

"*Don't you do it!*" the scorched thing gurgled yet again—this crisped and peeling, bodiless, agonized visage—hanging there like an apparition in the dark. "*Don't you dare do it!*"

Its hair smoked, burned away from one half of a blistered scalp. Its left eye was a gaping, blackened hole in a scorched and peeling roast of a face whose seared cheekbone was clearly visible. Its mouth was welded shut in the corner on that side, causing its withered lips to writhe as they issued its urgent, stilted, inexplicable warning:

"*Don't do it! You mustn't…mustn't…do it!*"

And finally I was able to swallow, to squeeze saliva into my throat and moisten it, and choke the question out. "What is it that…that I mustn't do? I mean, what do you want of me? What are you asking?"

At which the thing—this ruined face, this apparition—twitched, blinked its good eye and despite its awful injuries somehow managed to assume a bewildered expression as it slowly backed away. And emboldened I called after it, "Wait a moment. Don't go. What is it you don't want me to do?"

But then its attitude seemed to change, to harden. For a moment it hung there in midair, gazing at me intently through that one good eye. And as I in turn tried to back off—which needless to say I couldn't, because one can't in nightmares of this sort—so the thing rushed upon me, angry now, frustrated that it wasn't getting through to me or because it didn't know how to. And as I tried to ward it off:

"*Don't!*" it shouted, spitting blood and yellow pus in my face as frustration split its welded lips, and strips of seared skin curled like wafer-thin shavings down its chin. "*Don't you do it!*"

Its voice was full of pain, and its teeth were white, red and clenched; they were grinding where they showed through that fretted left cheek!

Which is when I woke up screaming, screaming my lungs out, and I'm not ashamed to admit it....

After that…thankfully the nightmare's incidence in this its most recent, more grotesque form was only sporadic, and by chance or sheer good fortune I was seventeen before it once again came to the notice of my parents. By then, however—having scared the wits out of my mother one night with my gibbering and shrieking—I had decided it was time to reveal the extent of my problem and perhaps seek help.

By then, too, I had submitted four extremely well-received scientific papers and had been assured a position in one of the country's finest experimental labs when my formal education was complete, and I knew the last thing that any future colleagues of mine would want to discover— or that I would be prepared to reveal—was that since my childhood through young manhood I had been suffering from…well, how best to put it? A deep-seated persecution complex? Mental depression? Some rare psychological disorder? Any or all of these things? Possibly.

I saw several shrinks (please excuse my use of this term, and try to understand: I've never had much faith in psychiatry, so this was somewhat of an ordeal for me), one of whom went so far as to attempt regression. Perhaps my cynicism was to blame for his total failure; or perhaps it was simply that there was nothing in my past, my childhood, that he could focus in on or pinpoint as the source of any emotional problem whatsoever.

And so, not knowing when it would strike next, I was left to suffer the nightmare, all through my final term of education and well into my nineteenth year, when mercifully its fortnightly, then monthly, then quarterly incidence seemed to indicate a gradual remission. So that by the time I took up my position at "the facility" (whose location I may not reveal for reasons of national security) I had again begun to believe that perhaps this time my troubles were truly behind me—

—When in fact they were ahead....

The facility.

While I may not reveal its location—for fear of making it a prime target in any future conflict—its purpose isn't any longer a matter of national security. Indeed, and for the last decade, a majority of the world's technologically advanced countries have been engaged in just such research.

As for the research in question:

Wasn't it Einstein himself who declared the concept of a past, a present, and a future—the concept of time, in fact—an illusion, albeit a persistent one? That at least was the substance of it if not in so many words. Temporal physics, yes, dizzying even by quantum standards. But as to why anyone would *want* to travel through time, to speed up their passage through it, or indeed reverse it....

Well, I shall risk my status as a citizen and a hero and propose one of my own theories. Wouldn't it be a good idea to slide a century or so back down the space-time cone and adjust history somewhat, just a tweak here and there? No of course it wouldn't! And I know that any reasonable, reasoning mind would recoil in sheer terror at the notion. Ah, but tell that to the government, and to those military men who believe that a world without Hitler—a world which had never known men such as Mao or Osama, or a hundred others of that ilk—would be a better world. Perhaps they are right, but what if they are wrong? At least the world we know is stable, the status quo maintained.

But of course I'm only guessing (despite the presence of the CIA and certain uniformed types in an allegedly "advisory" capacity.)

And so at just twenty-one years of age—and because we all have to earn our keep—that is where I had been working for two years and some months when my nightmare manifested yet again in its final, most monstrous form and at the worst possible, indeed the *only* possible, time....

★ ✦ ★

The facility's Powers That Be had eventually decided, despite what I've said above, that the past was forbidden and nothing physical could be made to materialize there. They had reasoned that if it were at all possible it would have already happened; surely we would have sent something into the past, and, knowing in advance what we were *going* to do would have been witness to its arrival—which is an indication of how far ahead we were with the project— which in turn is to say that we were ready. Or ready for the future, at least.

Only then—if we could get that far and send some object a few minutes into the future—would we reconsider the past. As to the time-traveler in question: since earlier experiments had indicated that a non-metallic element would have the first best chance, the subject of our experiment was to be a simple glass paperweight.

I was to be the last one out of the vault, the one making the final minute, feathery adjustments to the equipment. But of course I can't describe the equipment, not if I'm interested in preserving my heroic image and citizenship.

And there I was alone of humanity in that vast underground lab, me and the machine. And I must say I felt oppressed by the sheer weight of protective lead surrounding me on all sides—protecting those on the *outside*, that is—yet at the same time excited by the knowledge that much of this, not only the theory but also in large part the actual design of the experiment, was the product of my own imagination and creativity.

Oppressed yet excited…but was it only the lead shielding I felt weighing upon me? And might not my excitement in fact be fear? But fear of what: the possible consequences of what I was about to do? Suddenly I felt oddly perverse: I sensed a danger, yet welcomed it! But there again, was Einstein perverse when he formulated his most famous equation, $E=mc^2$? No, neither man nor equation…not even in the searing light of Hiroshima. Science is science, after all. And as for me: I was no Frankenstein….

But finally we were ready; my monitors and meters were displaying optimum readings, and outside the vault my colleagues—in fact *my* team—were reading their own monitors, conversing excitedly, and beckoning me to join them beyond the reinforced carbon-crystal portholes.

Which was when I felt the darkness swirling and knew that it was happening again; not a nightmare this time but a *waking* horror, a daymare! Again it had come to plague me. I was awake, yes, yet must have seemed half-asleep to those who watched me; asleep and staggering in the grip of invisible forces, swaying like a zombie, mesmerized by this thing which only I could see:

That tortured, fire-blasted face forming out of a darkness conjured in my mind. But more than a face this time, this last time…a face, a neck, and the upper half of a torso, all of it ravaged and worse than ravaged. The left arm had been torn free of a shoulder that spurted blood, spattering the apparition's laboratory smock. But…a laboratory smock?

And finally I understood, knew what it was all about, what it had always been about. Which was perhaps the most staggering revelation of all. So that even as the thing gibbered its first and last warnings at me— "*Don't do it! You mustn't do it!*"—I was passing out, my mind refusing to take it in, shriveling in upon itself like an abruptly deflating balloon.

I remember stumbling against a laboratory table, trying to grasp it and steady myself, and the experiment's remote control device falling from my suddenly spastic fingers…then of its landing face-down, of course, on the button, and so triggering the experiment.

With me inside the cone zone.

Then the blast like a great bomb going off in my face, the wash of alien heat lifting me up and taking me with it, and the pain that I felt without really feeling it. No, for I must have been half out of it before…well, before I was out of it.

But it's possible that I remember one other thing: wondering whose arm it was, spraying blood as it went spinning across the laboratory floor…?

As for the glass paperweight:

I'm told it disappeared, only to reappear a minute or so later as a scattering of perfectly formed clear glass marbles of various sizes, which blinked out of sight before they could roll off the smoking laboratory table…materializing a week later as a clump of silicon crystals before disappearing again…and reappearing after four months as a small heap of glass dust, then at once vanishing…to return in a three-month as an acidic vapor that blinded the technician who had been left in charge of the obviously ongoing experiment.

Since when there has been nothing.

So while time travel is possible, we still have a long way to go before we'll have even a short *time* to go! But I believe we'll succeed in the end. And while I'm no longer able to give of myself physically, my mind is still keen…indeed, only a very small part of it has escaped me…

So then, what had happened?

Well as anyone with even a basic schooling in science will know, every action has a reaction. I had sent something of the paperweight into the future, its elements if not its structure. But since time is kept in balance by space, the spacetime universe had reacted, compensated. And I was the one in the cone zone.

My mind, or something of my mind (certain of its elements at least) had been blasted down the time-cone into the past, aware that it had an urgent warning to impart if not what the warning was about. And for thirteen years or thereabouts that dazed *thought* had been visiting its former habitation, trying now and then to warn me of my deadly future, but ever fading and losing coherency—

Until the time when I first dreamed the thing, when I was just eight or nine years old; dreamed of the face—*my future face*—before the fragment sped off into an even earlier time, when there had been no me to warn....

★ ✦ ★

Feasibility Study

So then, here's me writing this Science Fiction stuff and as of yet I haven't even managed to get off the planet! I've put some peculiar things on planet Earth but I haven't yet sent anything or anyone off into space... not too far, anyway. Well, "Feasibility Study" puts that right, as do the two tales that follow it and close out the book.

Written in November/December, 2004—just a month ago as I sit writing this—it's one of my two most recent tales, and in its way has turned into something of a moral story, even though that wasn't my original intention. Much like "The Strange Years" and "The Man Who Felt Pain," it makes, I think, a strong case for conservancy.

And before you ask: no I'm not a Green... or a blue, black, purple or gray either. And I'm certainly not a pink. But you'll see what I mean....

I

From the *Journal of Laurilu Hagula*, 2nd Engineer,
United Earth grav-drive vessel *Starspike Explorer*
out of Darkside Luna, Earthdate 2nd January, 2403.

Ophiuchus VIII Equivalents, Earth standard:

Diameter...............0.875 approx.
Day...............0.875 approx.
Mass...............0.889 approx.
Atmos................Breathable.
Life...............Varied, non-sentient.

"I have always had problems with this 'non-sentient' thing. According to my antique dictionary, which was published in the last decade of the 20th Century, the adjectival sentient means: 'conscious, capable of sensation; aware, or responsive to stimulus. While paradoxically (or so it seems to me), as a noun it bears the description, 'sentience, that which is sentient; as a sentient *being or mind*—my italics. A contradiction in terms, it seems—or perhaps a contradictionary? I mean, does a plant have a mind? As a vegetarian, that concerns me.

"Ophiuchus VIII is not the first world on which I have come up against this paradox. But then, neither is it unknown on the home world, planet Earth. Is a squirting cucumber sentient? Is a scallop? Is that shrub (I can't remember its name, but then I'm no botanist) whose myriad leaves on all the neighboring bushes close up in apparent distress if just one leaf feels the artificial heat of a struck match?

"The first (my dictionary says it's a cucurbitaceous plant, native of Earth's Mediterranean regions) forcefully ejects ripe seed pods when it 'senses' footfalls or 'feels' an animal brushing against it. Well, it's certainly not 'aware'—but 'responsive to stimulus?' As for the scallop: it is, after all, only a bivalve, having a shell in two parts. But it also has rudimentary eyes, a good many, and avoids oceanic predators by clapping its valves and 'swimming' away from them. And we (human beings, that is) have been eating them for untold thousands of years.

"So then, these things are patently mindless—they have no appreciable brains; and, in the botanical examples as specified above, none whatsoever—but they do respond to stimuli. This is my problem, and confronted by Ophiuchus's javelin-hurling tree ferns, I thank goodness I am not the ship's exobioecologist!

"One other thing about the tree ferns: they sing, and when 'hurt' they wail. I have heard their wailing and it is painful; or perhaps pain-filled? In future I shall follow the example of my Number One: leave the forest well alone and stick to tending my engines...."

II

RESTRICTED! RESTRICTED! RESTRICTED!
Non-electronic. By hand only!

ANOMALY 13: Preliminary Report.

By: Helmut W. Silberstein Jr.
Comdr United Earth Station IV.
Dated: 5th Aug. 2407.

To: Security List "A" only.
Non-electronic. By hand only!

Retrospective:

Of the 12 previous so-called "anomalies" recorded since United Earth Station One was commissioned in 2297, one was a disintegrating comet whose fragments fell into the sun; three were NEOs (Near Earth Objects) of which only one came inside Luna's orbit; six were "drifting scrap iron"—debris left over from the various "space races" prior to planetary reconciliation and harmonization—since dismantled, assisted into decaying orbits, and allowed to burn up in atmosphere; one was a quarter million tons of rock and ice on a collision course with Earth, atomized by massive nuclear bombardment from Titan Base; and No. 12 was detected, observed and recorded by a robotic early warning buoy for a period of six days Earth standard in an apparently stable orbit around Venus. It then removed or disappeared...this was some three years and four months ago.

In every respect this penultimate anomaly—No. 12, which was more properly an *anomaly* in the truest meaning of the word, not merely a means of reporting (usually) NEOs—was identical to the subject of the following report, namely **ANOMALY 13**. This did not become a proven fact until midway through the following sequence. However, in any event, my course of action would have been no different as the exploration and investigation of space is the approved business of the United Earth Space Agency and I am a Commander of that organization....

REPORT

Sir, I have to report that:

At approx 2340 Hrs. 1st Aug. 2407 I was the Officer in Command of UES IV, in a stable orbit over the North Atlantic, when Anomaly 13 was detected, a) by onboard radar, and b) manually, telescopically, some seven kilometres in advance of the UES in a corresponding orbit.

At approx 2347 Hrs, when it was observed that the anomaly's proximity had narrowed to six kilometers, I authorized a manned shuttle approach a) to determine the nature of the anomaly, and b) to remove any obstruction in the event it should prove to be "orbital junk," or c) to take it aboard the shuttle and eventually the UES for atmospheric inspection and investigation if it should prove to be of obscure or unknown origin.

I then computer-encoded a message and in addition used the scrambler to inform Space Central Arizona of my actions so far, with which the Officer-on-Watch readily concurred.

Shuttle pilot James Goodwin with co-pilot Susannah Rafferty launched in Shuttle One at 2358 Hrs approx. Meanwhile Astrotech 1st Class Andre Galante had got the computers back on line following a period of sporadic sunspot interference and completed a comparison with the aforementioned Venus-orbiting anomaly.

About 0004 Hrs, 2nd Aug., Goodwin reported on the nature of the extra-terrestrial vessel. It was:

1) Pyramidal with four triangular sides, any of which could be said to be the base. Measured from the base or bases to apex or apexes, the vessel was some eight feet in length.

2) It was made of a dull silvery metal—possibly silver or nickel-silver, or a similar alloy.

3) It showed no sign of damage or long-time exposure to the void, and had gathered no dust despite that it possessed a weak magnetic field.

4) It had triangular "windows" of a material which at first appeared transparent, possibly reinforced glass or crystal, set centrally in each facet. The windows reflected moon, starlight, and the shuttle's inspection beams dazzlingly.

6) One of these windows was located in what could well have been a triangular hinged hatch.

I then relayed this information on scrambled to Space Central, along with live-action footage from Shuttle One. The Officer-on-Watch double-checked with all relevant agencies that the vessel was not a) one of theirs, and b) that it was not a previously uncharted weapon left over from the 20th Century's space race. Acting on instructions from Space Central, I then authorized EVA from Shuttle One, and at approx 0023 Hrs pilot Goodwin and co-pilot Rafferty exited their shuttle to initiate a closer examination of the (probably) alien vessel.

Why both of them? Because this being, in all likelihood, an historic occasion—the first proof of ET intelligence, namely contact with an alien artifice or vessel of a spacefaring species—one hundred per cent corroboration of all activity would be required, including pictures. Using extreme caution, Goodwin would approach the vessel and attempt to look in through one of its windows, while Rafferty photographed and performed a commentary on his activities. Both of them were tethered to and life-supported by Shuttle One, of course. And I had already launched Shuttle Two for backup.

As to what next happened: we have photographic footage from the automatic camera on Shuttle One; also the statements of the crew of Shuttle Two, who were fast approaching point rendezvous when the incident occurred. In addition, we have a recording of Rafferty's commentary—or more properly her conversation with Goodwin—up to the point of termination.

As a reminder I append a transcript of the last few seconds of that conversation, as follows:

TRANSCRIPT

Rafferty: "Jim, what's the mass of that thing, you reckon?"

Goodwin: "That's hard to say, Sue. It looks kind of flimsy, though. I'll have a better idea of how solid it is after grabbing hold of it, which I must if I'm going to take a look in one of those windows."

Rafferty: "Okay, as long as it doesn't set you spinning. Go easy, won't you, Jim?"

Goodwin: "It isn't tumbling fast enough to trouble me much, and in any case I think I can take a couple revolutions without throwing up—and my jetpack is working just fine. Sue, are you worried about me or something?"

Rafferty, laughing: "No, not really. It's just that I think you're dizzy enough already!"

Goodwin, laughing: "Okay, stand off and get some good shots of this. I'm going to grab the next apex as it swings on by me. A case of one small touch for man, one fantastic grope for mankind! Here goes, and…*Whoah!*"

Rafferty, anxiously: "Jim, what's wrong?"

Goodwin: "Wrong? Oh, nothing. Just that this thing seems to be weightless, is all. Might as well be a paper bag! Brought it to a halt just like that! Now I'm taking hold of the raised rim on the hatch, if that's what it is, and—"

Rafferty: "Jim?"

Goodwin: "I'm, *uh*, trying to look in through the window. It looks like glass or maybe crystal—it *looks* transparent, too—but isn't. Maybe it's frosted up. The glitter is blinding. Like a mess of diamonds. Can you come in a little closer? If we both use our torches together…"

Rafferty: "Here I am. Move over a bit."

Goodwin, chuckling: "How come we've never got this close in atmosphere, like on board the UES?"

Rafferty: "'Cos it's against regulations, that's why. Ready with your torch?"
Goodwin: "Okay. Lights, action, camer*aaggghhhh!*"

END OF TRANSCRIPT

Less than six hundred metres away from rendezvous at that time, (0030 Hrs), the copilot of Shuttle Two recorded what he could see of the contact between his colleagues and the alien vessel. Also, the camera on Shuttle One was continuing to function, and thus both observed and corroborated the facts of the matter. As Goodwin and Rafferty shone their torches in through the window, either a) the beams were reflected blindingly, or b) the vessel itself emitted an intense and all-encompassing light. This took the form of a single dazzling "flash," as opposed to continuous illumination, and when the light returned to normal—which it did immediately—Goodwin, Rafferty, and the alien vessel were no longer there. Together with so-called "Anomaly 13," the crew of Shuttle One had disappeared; their life support tethers were subsequently found to have been sheared through as by an incredibly sharp cutting instrument that left no marks or indication of forceful laceration.

There was no debris, neither human nor artificial, as would be expected in the aftermath of a massive explosion; no detectable radiation; nothing to indicate the whereabouts of the vanished persons and artifice or explain their disappearance....

Sir, I have stated as best possible the terrible facts of the matter. Now, as the Commander of United Earth Station IV—in the sure knowledge that without their shuttle's life support systems Goodwin and Rafferty would have something less than two hours to live, and the fact that they have been listed "missing in the performance of their duties" for over seventy-five hours now—I take this early opportunity to request a) that Shuttle One be adorned with a commemorative plaque recording the names and relevant details of its crew and their demise, and b) that the shuttle itself be enabled to remain permanently in orbit as a most suitable mausoleum and monument to these most honorable astronauts.

And I remain, sir—
—Your Most Obedient Servant,
Helmut W. Silberstein Jr.
Comdr UES IV.
5th Aug 2407.

III

From the *Notebook of Michael Gilchrist*,
exobioecologist aboard United Earth grav-drive vessel
Starspike Explorer, Earthdate 4th January, 2403.

"Really must have words with the Captain, keep this bloody woman off my back! A vegetarian, vegan or whatever? God, but if she keeps this up she'll be living on hay and water and nothing else! Why hay? Because on an untamed, unsettled planet where as yet there are no herbicides, combined harvesters or lawnmowers, namely Ophiuchus VIII, hay is grass that has died naturally and dried out in the sunlight, in other words, we 'cruel exobioecological types' can't be accused of torturing it first! And come to think of it, I have probably just prescribed the perfect diet for the silly cow! And as for water—so-called 'pure' water—I'm tempted to point out to her that every time she takes a sip she's sending countless innocent microscopic organisms to their soupy graves in her own acid-bath digestive system!

"She has a problem, she says, with the wailing. Well *I* have a problem every time the *Starspike Explorer* wobbles into or out of grav-drive. *I* have a problem trying to understand how we can hook up on ripples in subspace that have their source in stars that went bang billions of years ago. I've got neither the math nor the right kind of mind for it, which is why I keep the hell out of the engine-room: because that place frightens me just as much and probably more than the Ophiuchus foliage—namely the tree ferns—frightens her.

"It's the tree ferns, yes….

"Well, actually, they don't frighten her…it's just that she's sorry for them! But all of Ophiuchus's greenery is weird. I keep trying to tell her it's a young world, and Nature hasn't quite sorted it out yet. We have plants on Earth that look like animals, and animals that look like plants; that's just evolution, is all. And it's the same here, except things are evolving somewhat differently. Here it turns out the flora and fauna are just a tad more like each other. But sentient? Hell no! No such thing. And man cannot live by bread alone, especially when he's eighty light-years from a wheat field!

"Ophiuchus VIII:

"There's a little less oxygen in the air: 20.2 percent, and a little less nitrogen: 77 percent; with swamp methane, carbon dioxide, argon, neon and the usual suspects soaking up another 2.65 percent, along with a smidgeon of krypton, zenon, and like that. And yes, I know I'm far too casual, too familiar with all of this stuff, but I'm *never* contemptuous of it; not like Laurilu Nagula when she takes it out on an inoffensive gravimonitor with a twelve-inch monkey-wrench in mid-drive!

"Anyway, putting her out of mind if not her misery, *which I might yet*—

"—Ophiuchus VIII:

"It took us eighteen months to get here and when we're done it will take us another eighteen months to get back. But that's no big deal really, not when you come to consider it. If I remember my history correctly, didn't it take Christopher Columbus just as long to get to America and back to Spain? He called his discovery the New World but it was never a new planet—and he certainly didn't have to sail across eighty light-years of deep space in order to discover it! But there I go again....

"My problem: I'm too easily distracted. I have a butterfly mind, or so they tell me. It flits hither and thither. Thither: a damn silly word. Say it often enough, quickly enough, it soon becomes meaningless. Thither, thither, thither.

"See what I mean? So where was I? Ah, yes:

"Since the discovery of the gravity drive ninety years ago humanity has been spreading out—but actually we're spreading inwards, sideways, and up and down—throughout the Milky Way galaxy; more properly throughout our spiraling arm of the galaxy. But since the Milky Way is a hundred thousand light-years across, even with the propulsive energies of dead stars giving us a push we've a long, long way to go yet.

"So why are we here—I mean out here, on Ophiuchus VIII?

"Well, while stars like Sol are fairly common, planets like the Earth are few and far between. And the Earth is ecologically moribund, overpopulated, no longer able to supply its people with fossil-fueled energy or even sufficient good, clean food. In a nutshell and while yet there *are* such things as nuts, it's way past time we moved house. Back on Earth the population can, must, will be controlled, and maybe in another hundred years there will be room to move and breathe again. But we cannot let mankind stagnate, go into decline, die; and out here, if we can find new planets to tame, settle, populate, then the human race can blossom all over again, explode throughout space, and eventually, even if it takes millennia, become literally universal.

"Personally I'm of the belief that this was Old Ma Nature's plan in the first place. I see the Earth as a nest and humanity as the nestlings. That's us, what we've been: fledglings bumping about in our nest. And Ma Nature, the mother bird, has been trying to feed us as fast as our greedy little beaks could snap up the food she's regurgitated. But the bigger and the stronger we got the more we bumped around, until we just about shook the nest to pieces. We shook it, shit in it and fouled it up generally, until it could no longer support us. And the mother bird, Ma Nature, finally said, "Okay you lot, it's time to fly. I've been a good mother but now you must fly away and build your own nests, your own worlds." And that's what we're doing.

"But as for what I said about the home world—how maybe in a hundred more years it will be viable again—who do I think I'm kidding? The fact is it's done, burned out, finished…I was never so happy to get the hell out of it! And that's why I became an *exo*bioecologist; because the way I see it there's no future in Earth ecology.

"Okay, I realize that if I *was* an ecologist back on planet Earth I'd probably be burned at the stake for what I just wrote. But that's because hope springs eternal and they're all hanging on in there, hoping they can turn things around. Some hope! But me: I'm an *exo*bioecologist, out here where Old Ma Nature intended me—intends us, humanity—to be, building our new nests on new worlds….

"So then…why am I writing all this stuff when I should be finishing my feasibility study and working on a report? Answer: because a silly vegetarian bitch who worries about wailing tree ferns has irritated the hell out of me, that's why! God, I should never have gotten into conversation with her! She understands as much about alien life-forms as I do about her gravity drive engines—nothing!

"But on the other hand…well, some of the things Laurilu has said have sort of stuck in my mind. And once again *if* I was a Green—an ecologist on Earth—I would probably agree with certain of her arguments. Hell no, I *know* I'd agree with them—it's just that they're a few hundreds of years too late, that's all!

"Okay, okay, let's put her out of mind, but definitely, and try to work up some notes toward my feasibility report….

IV

RESTRICTED! RESTRICTED! RESTRICTED!
CLASSIFICATION: EXTREMELY URGENT!

ANOMALY 13: Secondary Report.

By: Helmut W. Silberstein Jr,
Comdr United Earth Station IV.
Dated: 12th Aug. 2407,
Time: 1032 Hrs.

To: Security List "A" only.

Retrospective:
Sirs, see my preliminary report, dated 5th Aug. 2407, in particular my request in re honoring the crew of Shuttle One out of UES IV.

While this was under consideration by Higher Command, I was ordered to recover Shuttle One into a secured bay aboard UES IV where a series of exhaustive tests were to be carried out by an investigative team out of Space Central Arizona. The investigative team would launch today at 1400 Hrs and rendezvous with UES IV at 1540 Hrs.

In the light of further developments—made specific in the report which follows—I now respectfully request that the investigation be held in abeyance and that a medical team replace the investigators. UES IV does have its own doctors, of course, but we lack a) a forensic pathologist, and b) a qualified psychoanalyst....

REPORT

Sirs, I have to report that:

About one hour ago, at approx 0930 Hrs, the automatic alarm in Shuttle Bay Five—the secured bay where Shuttle One is held in isolation awaiting inspection and investigation—was activated by a then unknown agency.

Despite that the UES's sensors had failed to indicate any impact, and at first suspecting a hull breach, probably of meteoric origin, in accordance with Station SOPs I ordered a team to suit-up in order to enter the bay and investigate the occurrence. However, when it was observed that the computers had not registered any abnormal loss of atmosphere, I belayed the suit-up order and instead sent in the UES's Rapid Reaction Team as a precautionary measure. All of this in just a few brief minutes.

Then, even as the seals on Bay Five's hatch were removed, a garbled communication in the form of an SOS—a cry for help on a space-suit's frequency—was received from within the bay; in fact from the vicinity of isolated Shuttle One. Patched through to me by the Station's Radio Op, the voice was unmistakably Jim Goodwin's. We do have a recording; suffice it to say that shuttle pilot Goodwin's message was barely coherent and punctuated by much foul language. Also, he sounded utterly exhausted.

Within Bay Five and close to Shuttle One, both Goodwin and copilot Susannah Rafferty were discovered naked and in a mutilated condition. Their pressure suits lay nearby; pilot Goodwin had used his to make the call for help. Rafferty was dead, in a state of rigor mortis, and Goodwin was unshaven and hysterical. Moreover, the mutilations that the pair have suffered, of which Rafferty would appear to be the principal victim, are grotesque in the extreme. On that subject I cannot find words to properly express my feelings; the visuals that accompany this report may explain my reticence in this respect, also the urgency of medical/psychological assistance.

Sirs, I can offer no reasoned explanation for anything that has occurred here, other than to stake my reputation as a Commander of the Space Agency on this being the work of inimical ET intelligences.

And at 1047 Hrs, 12th Aug. 2407, I remain—

—Your Most Obedient Servant,

H. W. Silberstein Jr.

Comdr UES IV.

V

Journal of Laurilu Nagula,
2nd Engineer, United Earth grav-drive vessel
Starspike Explorer. Earthdate: 5th Jan. 2403.

"Hateful though I find it, still I couldn't resist it. So today I went out again to watch them—if only for a minute or two—at their work. 'Them': Mike Gilchrist and his crew. Exobioecologist Gilchrist, who styles himself 'a 25th Century Darwin, but far more important than the original.' His reasoning: Gilchrist is not so much concerned (he says) with cataloging a multitude of species as with preserving one in particular—mankind! Egotistical bugger! But...I suppose in a way he's right. That is why we're here.

"Anyway, decked out in boots and protective clothing I went out into the forest to where the tree ferns flourish. From some two hundred yards away I could hear them beginning to wail, and I knew that Gilchrist and his gang of—but no, I shouldn't say it, shouldn't call them butchers; there, I've said it anyway—knew that they were stripping a tree.

"The wailing...makes my flesh creep. Mournful? It's quite literally a dirge! Yet despite that I'm caused to cringe at the sound I'm reminded of the squirting cucumbers and of that shrub back on Earth with the heat-sensitive leaves. They are not—I mean *definitely not*—sentient. So why should I feel so passionately for the tree ferns? Or could it possibly be that I'm more truly ecologically-minded than Gilchrist?

"Damn! But there I go again, torn two ways. We're here, and we must eat. Not us especially, not the thirteen-member crew of *Starspike Explorer*, but those who will follow us to settle Ophiuchus VIII, which of the several worlds we and our four sister ships have visited so far is *by* far the most eminently suitable for colonization. So says Michael Gilchrist, and of course he's right. No terraforming necessary, or very little, and plenty of fresh water. At 30.9 ft per sec^2, the equatorial gravity is just a touch less than Earth standard, and we have an acceptable atmosphere. Also—and most importantly—the soil will support a good many terrestrial trees, cereals, and other food crops; which in turn will support plenty of animal species. As a result, the barest minimum of terraforming that's required will be achieved 'naturally.' And yet more importantly—*far* more importantly—there already exists an ample supply of food here….

"…Which brings us back to the tree ferns.

"Gilchrist was sitting on a rock well back from the action, outside the range of the javelins. Actually, they are more like darts or small arrows; it was me who dubbed them javelins after the definition from my antique dictionary: 'javelin, a throwing spear.' And for a fact the tree ferns do throw them. I was just in time to witness that for myself when one of Gilchrist's crew fell victim to the fact. He was standing arms akimbo within the radius of fire, from which location he watched three colleagues at work, when suddenly he yelped, jumped six inches in the air, and fell on his backside clutching his right knee. And:

"'Shit!' the squat, bearded Gilchrist grumbled. 'See that? Took a javelin in the knee. That's another man in the sick bay, knee swollen up like a puffball for at least a week, maybe ten days. Three down and three to go. *Shit!*'

"I was surprised because Gilchrist's man was wearing protective clothing—his 'armor'—no less than me and Gilchrist. But as his man came staggering and cursing, the exobioecologist explained: 'The barbs on the tips of these things are flexible, a sort of cartilage. Instead of bouncing off this light-weight armor they slither along it into the first available joint.'

"'A typical example of non-sentience?' I lifted an eyebrow at him. I knew that I wasn't only wrong but that I also exacerbated matters by enjoying all of this, of course. Indeed, that was the point of my remark: it pleased me to irritate him.

"'A simple response to stimuli!' He snapped. 'Also, it's a typical example of exoevolution. These little armadillo things that chew on the tree ferns—these rat-sized woodlice—they are armor-plated too. Now answer me this: why do blackberries have thorns, eh?'

"'Earth brambles?' I shrugged. 'To keep the birds off?'

"He shook his head. 'Birds eat the fruit, carry the seeds, shit them out miles away so propagating the plant. No, in point of fact the bramble favors birds like flowers favor bees. The thorns are to ward *animals* off—including men—and keep them from trampling the vines. Much like your Mediterranean, squirting bloody cucumbers.'

"'So what do I know?' I said. 'You're the ship's exobioecologist!'

"'Would be,' he said, 'if people would stop interfering and bloody well let me get on with it!'

"Pale behind his visor and limping quite badly, Gilchrist's wounded man reached us. 'Goddamn thing shot me!' he said unnecessarily, staring at his leg where five or six inches of tufted javelin protruded from his armor's knee joint.

"'This may hurt a little,' Gilchrist told him, and without pause stooped to yank it out. The barb was stained red but the javelin was already wilting, drooping like a piece of wet spaghetti. The injured man shuddered and went paler still.

"'Go on back to the ship,' Gilchrist went on. 'Mildly poisonous, but Doc will give you a shot and you'll be okay. Can you make it on your own? Good.' And off the man staggered.

"Meanwhile one of his colleagues in the clump had commenced attacking the offending tree fern—with a flamethrower, of all things!

"'What on earth are you doing?' I screamed at them, as the tree fern began wailing and burst into flames.

"'Nothing, not on Earth,' Gilchrist answered for them.

"I might have rushed forward but the air was suddenly full of javelins. 'I mean, it's not as if you can *punish* the thing!' I yelled at them, stamping my foot. 'It's only a *plant!*' So why was I so inflamed?

"'Natural reaction,' Gilchrist told me, chewing his lip and looking just a little guilty. And for a moment I thought he was talking about *my* reaction. But no, he wasn't. 'Stinging nettles in your garden,' he went on, 'you cut 'em down. Poison-ivy, you burn it out. Hurt, you take revenge.' And he shrugged. 'Natural reaction.'

"By now the whole clump was wailing; maybe three dozen tree ferns, lashing the air with their fronds, releasing myriad javelins, sending a horde of squealing woodlice (which in fact are six-legged mammals that on the run look like nothing so much as chitin-plated meerkats, except they are herbivores and Ophiuchus VIII's dominant life-form) tumbling for their lives.

"But I had seen more than enough. Turning away, I caught up with Gilchrist's injured man and helped him back to the ship. I couldn't help hoping, though, that his shots were going to hurt like hell...."

VI

SESSION SEVEN.

Subject: James Goodwin,
former crew member United Earth Station IV.

Object: following eight weeks of (apparently) successful psychotherapy applied in order to eliminate a severe psychological blockage, to interview shuttle pilot Goodwin in relation to his experiences following abduction by unknown inimical extraterrestrial intelligences.
Interrogating Officer:
Dr. Gardner L. Spatzer,
Space Central, Arizona.
12th Oct. 2407.

RECORDED INTERVIEW

Dr. S: "Good morning, Jim!"
Goodwin, gloomily: "Yeah, sure."
Dr. S: "How are you feeling?"
Goodwin, nervous and agitated: "How do you suppose I'm feeling, Doc? Okay, I'll tell you—I feel like shit! Now maybe you can tell me something: do you intend to stick any more of those needles in me?"
Dr. S: "No, that shouldn't any longer be necessary—well, depending on your self-control. But if you should become excessively aggressive again...it was for your own good, Jim."
Goodwin, warily: "Okay, but be honest about it: do you have any needles on you, like right now?"
Dr. S, with a partly suppressed chuckle: "None whatsoever."
Goodwin: "Good! So I won't need to fight you off again...."
Dr. S: "Do you feel like talking now, answering some rather important questions?"

Goodwin: "You mean, am I *able* to talk about it? To tell you what happened to us? To tell the truth, I don't know...maybe. Do I *want* to talk about it? Hell no! But I might if you go easy on me. See, it's like the needles. Why do I fight them? Because if someone had stuck in your veins what they stuck in mine—in ours, mine and Susannah's—then you'd fight them the same as I do. You say I had a...a what? 'An extreme reaction?' Doc, the needles are just a very small part of it. But right now, if you were to show me a pin, a tack, or a nail—almost any-fucking-thing with a sharp point—then I can assure you you'd get the same reaction! *I mean, Jesus, it's...it's...it's—*"

Dr. S: "It's okay, Jim! Perfectly okay that you should feel upset. Perfectly natural. But do try to calm yourself down, and believe me when I tell you I understand."

Goodwin: "No, you don't. But okay, I'm calm. Perfectly calm now. So go right ahead, ask your questions. Only first I'd like you to answer one more of mine."

Dr. S: "I will if I can, certainly."

Goodwin: "I dunno, maybe you're not qualified. I mean, sure you're a mind doctor, but what I want to know is—I mean, it's not of the mind, at least I don't think so. It's sort of—"

Dr. S: "What, some physical thing? Relating to your current infirmity, perhaps?"

Goodwin: "That's right. It's like...I mean...I've heard it said that if you lose something...or things, like that—"

Dr. S: "—that you can still feel them?"

Goodwin: "Yeah."

Dr. S: "And can you?"

Goodwin: "No. Just the hurt, is all...."

Dr. S: "Well the hurting should stop—eventually. It's not like the mind, Jim. You *will* heal in time—which isn't to say that your mind won't, except that once again it will take time. Me, I only wish we *had* time or that we knew how long we've got. As for your physical pain: there are pain-killers, drugs, if it continues to trouble you. But don't let's forget the prosthetic they're working on; that will give you mobility and should help to take your mind off...things. You see, it's not like you're going to be helpless or confined or anything—not for too much longer, anyway."

Goodwin: "But as you just pointed out, Doc, it's not just a physical thing, not just physical pain. I mean, I remember now. When I relax and stop fighting it, I remember. *You* caused me to remember. And you know something? I should hate you for that. I should really fucking hate it that you've made me remember! You and your needles, and your questions, and all your *fucking psychobabble crap, and—*"

Dr. S: "Jim! Jim. you have to cut that out! We're past that now. You have to stop thinking for yourself, start thinking for your world. What you've got locked up in your head, we *need* it, Jim! We need you to tell us about it. You're an astronaut, Jim, one hell of a tough guy in a hell of a tough job. Which is why we know you can do this."

Goodwin: "Get it right. I *was* an astronaut, past tense."

Dr. S: "Well, I'm not going to lie to you; it must be obvious that we can't give you that back. But it's possible there's something almost as satisfying; perhaps something that will put everything else—most of everything else—right for you."

Goodwin: "Oh really? Like, you really think there is such a thing? Like what?"

Dr. S: "Like revenge! Why take it out on yourself, or on me and the others who are trying to help you, when you can take it out on them, the ones who did this to you?"

Goodwin, his voice suddenly shuddery, hoarse: "Them.... God, but you've never seen them! So cold, impersonal, inhuman, insensitive. We were—I don't know—nothing more than specimens, that's all. Bodies for biological or medical examination, dissection...*except we were alive!* You want me to remember? Oh, I remember all right! I only wish to God you would let me forget! I *want* to forget! But I can't, because every time I talk to you it's just like now. You make me...you make me...you *make* me fucking...rememmmmm...."

At which point Goodwin, traumatized, slipped back into what has become his safe haven, a comatose, psychoneurotic condition typified by severely restricted mental activity: a total neural shutdown. I am reasonably sure now that some unknown psychoactive agent has been introduced into Goodwin's system to prevent him from speaking about his ordeal; perhaps they didn't intend that he should talk about it. Nevertheless, I am encouraged to believe that we're making some progress, and I'm sure that the anticipated early delivery of Goodwin's prosthetic will accelerate the process.

Dr. Gardner L. Spatzer.

VII

From the *Notebook of Michael Gilchrist*,
exobioecologist aboard United Earth grav-drive vessel
Starspike Explorer, Earthdate 7th January, 2403.

"Knocked on the door of Laurilu's bunk last night.... Don't know why. Or maybe I do: wanted to apologize for what must have seemed my callous attitude out in the forest the other day. The fact is I'm not quite the unfeeling bastard she thinks I am.

"Anyway, and amazingly, she let me in! I thought maybe because she wanted to have it out with me—and that's *out* with me, by the way, not *off* with me!—which she did, and so did I, though to tell the truth neither one of us knew where to start.

"She had just opened a can of strawberry flavored juice—colored water, of course, with some added fizz—and asked me if I would like a drink. I accepted; we drank. And seeing a way to get through to her, I told her that only the fizz was real.

"At first she didn't know what I meant, then said, 'Oh, you mean the strawberries?'

"'Ain't no sech thang,' I said, 'not anymore. This is artificial flavoring, chemicals, that's all. Since the soft-fruit disease—what, seven years ago?—there aren't any soft fruit; well, except for the blackberries. They've been around forever; we never much tampered with them, and they're tough. But as for the rest of the soft fruit...you can forget it. It's a bug, a killer virus in the soil. But no way to kill it without killing the soil, which is three-quarters dead anyway.'

"'What?' she said, sitting up straighter and looking really good in her ship's uniform. 'I didn't know it was that bad.'

"'Why would you?' I said. 'You're the 2nd Engineer, not the expedition's ecologist, or bioecologist, or exobioecologist.'

"'Touché,' she said, not a little ruefully. 'But...you're saying *all* the soft fruits—all the berries, with the exception of brambles—saying they're gone forever? It's like, where have I been? I mean, I thought I was well up on all that stuff. How come I missed that? I *really* didn't know about it!'

"'People don't generally,' I told her. 'What, you think the World Health people, Calorie Control Council and food-rationing agencies—all the various Ministries of Agriculture, Farming, Fisheries, Hydroponics—you think they're likely to advertise the fact that the Earth is not-so-slowly dying, the air full of shit, the seas and lakes polluted, the ground poisoned?

I think not. *That* is why we're out here, Laurilu. Er, if you don't mind me calling you that?'

"'No, that's okay,' she told me, 'er, Mike?' And then continued: 'But that's the Earth you were talking about, while this is Ophiuchus VIII. Which—'

"'—which will soon be Earth II,' I cut her off.

"'Where we'll start—*have* started—the whole rotten process all over again?' She wasn't any longer sounding off…she just seemed a little sad, or a lot sad, as she slowly shook her head and continued, 'The destruction of a world, beginning with its inhabitants.'

"'You mean the tree ferns? They're just lettuces, cabbages, kale, Laurilu.'

"'But they wail when they're hurt!'

"'It's the wind in their fronds when they start in whipping them about, is all.'

"'And they hurl their javelins.'

"'Which is a result of them whipping their fronds! Because they evolved along with those meerrats or whatever you want to call them. But you know, if they could up roots and walk about, well! *I* wouldn't be any too happy about it either. Hell, I'm not especially happy about it anyway! But they're just plants—you even said so yourself.'

"Laurilu started to shake her head, then stopped and said, 'Yes I did. But still it seems to me that they protect themselves, even deliberately.'

"'The cactus has its spines,' I told her. 'What's more, and as well as deadly stinging tentacles, the Portuguese man-o'-war navigates the ocean's currents under sail. But not one of these species is equipped to *think* or do anything deliberately, Laurilu. They do things *automatically*, yes. But *deliberately*, no.'

"While I could see that I had her half-convinced, still she said, 'So what do we get out of a full-grown tree fern? I mean, pound for pound, dollar for dollar, are they worth it?'

"'Oh, yes!' On that I was positive. 'A full-grown tree? We get maybe nine gallons of sap. Add a little sweetener—it's as good as milk. Whip it, it's cream. Curdle it, it's cheese. Then there's the tender roots, of which there's almost as much below ground as above; maybe half a ton. And they're as good as potatoes. As for the fronds: they break down into fiber for textiles. The bark is thick but pliable: cork. And the wood…well it's wood, for burning. To settlers here the tree ferns will be like coconut-palms to the South-Sea islanders—when there *were* coconuts and South-Sea islands, that is.'

"'And when they've gone?' she said, staring at me, so that for the first time I noticed how beautiful her eyes are. 'After we've used them all up? What then?'

"'We won't use them all up. For every one we cut down we'll plant another. The only ground we clear will be for farming, to support us and whichever Earth livestock can thrive here. We'll put home-world fish into the lakes and oceans, put grass out on the creeper plains…we'll even have soft fruit again.'

"'Oh? How?' she said. I thought you said they were gone for good—or for bad.'

"I shook my head. 'No, I didn't say that. You said that. On Earth… they're probably gone for good, yes. We fooled around with them genetically and weakened them. We may even have introduced that virus into the soil, albeit accidentally. The breeds—all the exotics—they were the first to suffer. But we have seeds, shoots, cuttings, all carefully preserved or in hibernation, just biding their time, waiting to be planted in a little rich, living soil under some generous G-type sunlight.'

"She sighed her relief and said, 'Which means that when the first settlers get here—'

"'Which is only a few short years away, once we get back to Earth and I deliver my feasibility report.'

"'—that at least for a little while, and probably quite a while, they'll have to be vegetarians? Can I at least have that much to look forward to?'

"'Ah—not so.' Trying not to take too much pleasure in it, I shook my head. 'See, it's the general rule that if something eats something we eat, we can usually eat the first something. There are exceptions, of course, but….'

"Laurilu frowned and said, 'Come again?'

"And by way of explaining, I said: 'Those little, er, armadillo guys?'

"Her jaw fell open. 'Those little…but they're *animals*!'

"'That's right—and very nutritious, too. And what do you think cows, rabbits, goats, sheep and pigs are, Laurilu? And as for chickens…well, we'll have them all here, eventually.'

"Clenching her fists, she almost stood up. 'What do I think they are?" she said. 'I think they're *sentient*! Oh they may not think too good, but they *do* respond to stimuli…they do have brains, feelings—'

"'—And souls?' I got it in quick. 'Are you religious?'

"'What?' she said, caught a little off guard. 'Religious? I think so. My god may not be your god, but I don't believe everything is just accidental.'

"'Well me neither,' I said. 'And the Good Book tells us Man shall have dominion over all…We're *that* far above the other animals, that's all. We're almost as far above the home world's fauna as it is above the flora! So of course we eat it. Fish or fowl or four-legged beast, if it isn't poisonous we eat it! But we have to find that out first…which is what me and my team have been doing here on Ophiuchus VIII.'

"'But—'

"'But there's no but about it, Laurilu! Put it this way: do we just let humanity go to hell in a bucket along with the home world? No, of course not. It's us or the lesser species, kid.

"Again she shook her head, sighed, and said, 'Another world to ruin.'

"And I admit I nodded, sighed with her and said, 'Yes, only now we can do it a whole lot faster….' But I knew at once that I had made a mistake.

"Laurilu narrowed her eyes and said, 'We'll do what? How do you mean?'

"I shrugged, but not negligently, and answered, 'We managed to finish off the Earth in about—oh, I don't know—say four or five thousand years? But that was from our tribal beginnings to where we are now; from a time when the only fires were campfires to a time when we've sucked all of the black juice out of the ground and burned it in our cars, in heating our cities and powering our machines; from clean air and oceans to radioactive ruins and skies that leak dilute acid rains…. Are you with me so far?'

"'Go on,' she said, but very quietly now.

"'Ten years from now,' I said, just as quietly, 'they'll be sinking oil wells here. Twenty, there'll be towns, small cities. Twenty-five: airplanes and ocean-going liners, roads and tracks joining up the towns, motor cars on the roads and trains on the tracks. Another thousand years…well, by then we should have found Earth III, or IV, or even V. It's evolution, Laurilu. Mankind is evolving, expanding throughout the universe.'

"'And leaving precious little room for anything else,' she said.

"'But *is* there anything else?' I asked her then. 'We're it, as far as I can see. Where sentience is concerned, we're definitely it, Ma Nature's clever kids, Laurilu. The universe is our playpen, our schoolyard, our many worlds—all the places we're going to grow up in.'

"'You're saying that nature is so utterly uncaring, insensitive of the rest of her creations, that she's given us a whole universe to sack? All those stars and planets out here—or out there—and they're all for us? Only for us?'

"'That's how it appears,' I replied. Then I asked her: 'Did you ever hear of SETI?'

"'SETI?'

"'The Search for Extraterrestrial Intelligence,' I told her. 'SETI operated for over two hundred years sending radio signals out to the stars. Now we can get there faster than the signals! But you know what? There wasn't a single reply, not one. By now those signals have reached out over four hundred light-years in all directions, and no one out there gives a damn because there is no one out there. It'll take us two thousand years to get to all the places those signals have already left behind, where as far as we know there's nothing like us to compete with. So yes, it looks like it's all ours, Laurilu. If there is a god, we are his—or her—main men.'

"'Men *and* women.' She corrected me, shivering a little.

"So I put my arm around her, and she drew close. 'We're all there is,' I said. 'So we must make the best of what we've been given. Even of each other.'

"She pulled away just a little. 'But we haven't, we aren't, making the best of it. We're making a mess of it at the expense of everything we touch! And yet something you said has given me hope.'

"I smiled and pulled her in again. 'Now don't you start going soft on me, Laurilu!'

"She drew away again, quite suddenly, which caused the zipper on her uniform blouse to unzip two or three inches. But she didn't seem to notice. *I* noticed; after all this time away from Earth, well I was bound to. But just then it didn't occur to me that she'd been the same time away. And: 'No,' she said, 'don't distract me!' (Though I didn't know I had.) 'It's what you were saying about the tree ferns: how the settlers can use every bit of them. See, it's all the waste that I hate the most.'

"'The waste?'

"She was up on her feet in a moment; one pace of those long legs took her to her bookshelf…there's not too much room in a grav-ship's bunks. And: 'See,' she said again, 'when I got to know I was assigned to the *Starspike Explorer*'—she got down a book, one of her several antique volumes, and came and sat down again—'I decided to take at least an interest in every aspect of the expedition, which included ecology: planet Earth's ecology; or, as you might say, "when it had one." So I picked up a couple of old books on the subject. And this is one of them.'

"'Ah!' I said, nodding however reluctantly.

"'Even in those days there were people like me who deplored the waste,' she went on. 'And when you look at this you can see why. It's perfectly horrible!' Opening the book to a bookmarked page, she handed it to me. I knew at once what it was that Laurilu found so disturbing, and said:

"'Buying this was probably a mistake. An aunt of mine moved into an old house and explored the attic. She found a five-hundred-year-old book on human diseases—the *Compendium of Common Ailments & Household Cures*, or some such. And from that time on she had every disease you can name! If they were in the book my aunt got them, one at a time and often, or so it seemed, by the half-dozen! It was all in the mind. And you know what, Laurilu? She's still going strong at eighty-two! Still thinks she's sick, too.'

"She shook her head. 'But this isn't imagination. It really happened. Go on, look at it.' As she leaned to look at the book with me her zipper slipped an inch or two more. But like a fool I didn't look, except at the book. Well, mainly at the book.

"It was a picture of the bloody deck of a fishing boat. One of the fishermen had driven a long knife or machete through the head of a shark, almost nailing it to the deck, and another was slicing off its dorsal fin. There was a big basket full of fins to one side of the picture....

"And Laurilu said, 'It was the fins, Mike. They only wanted the fins...*to make soup!* The rest of the fish got tossed back in the ocean, and as often as not alive! Before that it was the whales, those huge great beasts, cut up alive for their livers, their oils. And those beautiful jungle cats—skinned for their furs. Ecology? On planet Earth? It was us, *we* murdered the home world, Mike! And we did it despite the warnings of *real* ecologists, like the man who wrote this book.'

"'Laurilu—' I began, without knowing how to continue. But as her arms crept round my neck it appeared that as suddenly as that her entire attitude had changed, and cutting me off before I could find any soothing or conciliatory words she went on:

"'Yet now—now like some kind of fantastic psychoanalyst or layer-on-of-hands—it seems that you've solved my problem, Mike! In giving me hope, you may even have cured me. It was the *waste* that was becoming my obsession, but now I see that it was just a part of everything that the human race does. Moreover, I think I know how to handle it now.'

"'And can you also see,' I said, taking her zipper all the way down, 'that we've simply got to make the best of what we've got? Get as much out of our short little lives as we can, while our hearts are still hammering and our blood still coursing? We—and now I mean you and me—we have to live our lives to the full, Laurilu, snatching at every opportunity we're given just as often and, er, as naturally as possible.'

"'Yes, I see that,' she answered, shrugging out of her uniform and assisting me with mine. 'And now maybe I'll be able to sleep without dreaming those dreams.' She began to bite my ear.

"'Dreams?' I repeated her, purely for the sake of something to say as we got down to business. 'About sharks, you mean?'

"'Well, that's one of them,' she answered between bites. 'I see them in my dream: unable to swim, dying and rotting away in their own environment, and not knowing how or why it happened.'

"'Exactly!' I told her. 'Not knowing how or why: non-sentient. And the reason the fishermen threw them back was so they'd go toward feeding other fishes, and them to feeding us. The sea was like—I don't know—like a big compost heap. The fishermen couldn't take those carcasses back to land where they'd rot and stink the place up, so they simply returned them to the sea where they had caught them, toppled them overboard into the big watery compost heap.' Our bodies were working in perfect unison now, becoming slippery as the temperature rose.

"'But there are other dreams,' she said, clawing at me spastically.

"'Oh, really? And what are they about, Laurilu?'

"'Well, there's one that's been bothering me quite a lot.'

"'And which one's that?' Actually, at that point in time, I couldn't have cared less.

"'The one where I look at the stars flickering by, and then look at the ship's engines, and find myself thinking that if we had never discovered the grav-drive, worlds like Ophiuchus VIII would be safe forever. But no, we'll soon be taking all of this knowledge, everything we've learned, back home with us. And me, I myself—Laurilu Nagula, Second Engineer—I'll be in *large* part responsible for bringing the *Starspike Explorer* home again in one…one piece.' She had gone quiet and thoughtful again, and had almost stopped moving under me.

"'But of course you will!' I groaned. 'And I'll be responsible for what I do, and likewise the rest of the crew: everyone responsible for the things they do.' Utter gibberish!

"'But now—' she came alive again, her hips powering, 'why, now *I* know my duty to…to everything! I know what I must do, Mike! You've helped me to realize that. But Mike?'

"'Yes?' I panted.

"'Please don't impregnate me.'

"'Don't worry about it,' I told her. 'Low sperm count. And anyway the radiation in your engine room will take care of what few tadpoles might manage to squirm through.'

"'My engine room, yes,' she whispered. 'It would seem to be the answer to everything.'

"'I'm glad I've been able to help you,' I told her. 'As for my feasibility report: well, you've also helped me. I can probably write it up from our conversation alone—without all the gloomy bits, of course.'

"'Do you think we can do this more often?' she said, sounding as sexy as anything I ever heard before, her need as strong as mine.

"'Often as you like,' I answered, my head beginning to buzz.

"'And on the way home, too?'

"'Absolutely!' (But wait a minute! Wasn't she beginning to sound just a little too serious?) 'Er, before we've been reassigned, split up, sent in our different directions, do you mean? Which of course we're almost certain to be.'

"'Something like that,' she said, her nails digging in just one last time. 'Before we...before we're split up and sent in our many different directions, yes.' But it was all babble now, meaningless babble as the sugar boiled over and began its melt-down onto our singing, soaring brains.

"Then, in a little while and after we had recovered, we did it again. Only this time without speaking. And I was especially satisfied because I'd not only had it *out* with Laurilu but *off* with her, too...."

VIII

NOTE:—On 12 Sept. 2405, having returned from exploring Ophiuchus VIII, and while attempting a landing at the Darkside Luna Base, *Starside Explorer* suffered a catastrophic failure of its engines. There were no survivors of the crash. While culpability—if such exists—is yet to be properly established, the ship's log and all shipboard books and documents have been recovered to Space Central, there to be studied, catalogued, and retained in the library's "restricted" archives until suitable excerpts can be released for general perusal and information....

IX

SESSION ELEVEN.
(Eleventh Week)

Subject: James Goodwin,
former crew member United Earth Station IV.

NOTE:— The fitting of Goodwin's prosthetic, just eight days ago, has had something of the desired effect. His spirits appear to have been substantially elevated and he is now far more positively receptive in respect of casual conversation.

As a direct result of Goodwin's massive loss of muscular tissue and skeletal support, however, his prosthetic adjunct—a device fashioned in an atmosphere of the utmost urgency—is of an unconventional, indeed unique design. An adaptation of a small power-loader's tractor, and equipped with a neural interface, a certain element of the grotesque was obviously unavoidable. Goodwin is aware that a lightweight and more esthetically pleasing model is currently under construction.

However, while Goodwin makes excellent physical progress by virtue of his renewed mobility and rapid mastery of his adjunct, his aversion to hypodermics and similarly sharp implements—symptomatic as it is of his extremely deep-seated psychosis—continues to be of great concern. And since the psychoactive drug Exaxavin is best delivered intravenously, it has now become necessary to introduce mild sedatives into his food as a means of premedication.

In general:

It appears that I was correct in my optimism regards ex-shuttle pilot Goodwin's prosthetic: the positive affect it might have on his well-being. We can now be fairly certain that in large part it was his loss of mobility—the sheer fact of his hospitalization and protracted recuperation, resulting in what must have seemed to someone of Goodwin's previous astronavigational skills, his agility, spatial coordination, and employment on the permanently low gravity United Earth Station IV, an interminable and claustrophobic confinement—it was that rather than his actual, physical truncation that was aggravating his mental condition and further delaying his recovery.

Therefore and in conclusion, I insist that the following transcript be read in the light of all the above information, and hasten to point out that despite the unsatisfactory culmination of the interview definite progress *is* being made as I probe ever more deeply into Goodwin's psychosis.

SPECIFICS: the following interview was recorded in Goodwin's quarters with the subject in a state of hypnotic regression, having reacted positively to an injection of fifteen milligrams of the drug Exaxavin. His trunk was upright in the upper frame of the prosthetic, giving him a standing elevation perhaps seven inches taller than my own. I therefore carried out the interview standing, the better to observe his expressions and speak to him "face to face," as it were.

Interrogating Officer:

Dr. Gardner L. Spatzer,

Space Central, Arizona.

3rd Nov. 2407.

RECORDED INTERVIEW

Dr. S: "Jim, do you remember where you were when last you heard my voice?"

Goodwin, without hesitation: "Sure. I was trying to look in through the window of this alien ship or probe, whatever it was. Couldn't see a thing—the glitter was blinding—which was odd because the sun was on the other side. Like it wasn't reflected light."

NOTE:— At this point during the *previous* interview, Goodwin had showed considerable irritability and signs of recovery from a seven milligram dose of Exaxavin. He was therefore instructed to sleep; and shortly, upon displaying normal REM, was awakened and the interview terminated.

CONTINUATION

Dr. S: "Well, that's where you are right now, trying to look in through the alien vessel's window. Can you see anything?"

Goodwin: "Nope, I'm still dazzled. But here comes Rafferty, so if I just give her a little room...there we go. She's something else, Susannah Rafferty: a really sweet thing. Damn it to hell, these pressure suits really piss me off! 'Hey, Sue—how come we never get this close aboard the UES, in atmosphere?'"

Dr. S: "And does she answer?"

Goodwin: "Yeah—something about regulations. And now she's got her flashlight ready. Maybe if we both shine our torches at this thing together the light will cancel out the dazzle. Okay, here we go. 'Lights, action, camera...*eh?*'"

Dr. S: "Jim? Are you okay? What's happening now?"

Goodwin, after a long pause: "Blinded! I'm blind as a fucking bat! And scared shitless! Weightless, too, but it's a different kind of weightlessness. And now...now I think I can see something. Yes, I believe I can see...something?"

Dr. S: "But where are you? What do you see?"

Goodwin: "This can't be real. I mean, I have to be dreaming this. I'm...I'm looking *down* on the universe—on everything—and its spinning like a top! It's like a globe of the Earth, except it's the whole damn universe...spinning. *Whoah!*"

Dr. S: "Jim, what is it?"

Goodwin: "Now it's stopped spinning and I think...I *think* I'm on the other side of...of the universe? And the light...there's that brilliant light again! A single flash of light...and now...the darkness returns. Utterly empty darkness; emptier than the void. I feel...nothing, no sensation whatsoever, it's like sleeping without dreaming, without even being asleep! Hard to explain or describe..."

Dr. S: "And the darkness? How long does this darkness last? Do you remember, Jim? Are you conscious in the darkness?"

Goodwin: "No idea. Weightless. Timeless. Totally lacking in any and all kinds of sensation. It's like...like I'm paralyzed in everything but my thoughts. I'm trying to call out to Sue...but it doesn't work. Nothing is working except my mind. And I'm thinking: maybe I'm badly hurt, in a sick-bay bed on UES IV. Some kind of trauma. But now—now, all of a sudden—all of a s-s-sudden...."

Dr. S: "Be calm now, Jim. It's okay. Everything is okay. So then, are you emerging from the darkness? Is that what's happening?"

Goodwin, becoming very agitated: "I...I think so. But...but I don't *want* to! And...and I'm not *going* to! I *won't*! So you can forget it, and I'll just stay right here in...in the d-d-dark."

Dr. S: "But Jim, I—"

Goodwin, arms and hands twitching, fists knotting, perspiration forming on forehead: "The darkness...is clearing. But I can't let it! Because I know...I know what's there behind it! I know...know...no...no...n-n-*oooooo*! Get the fuck away from me!"

Dr. S: "Jim! Listen to my voice now—"

Goodwin: his voice rising to another terrified shriek: "No, no, no, *noooooooooo!*"

(At this point Goodwin's arms began flailing, his hand inadvertently activating the neural interface switch situated on the console to his right. In short, as his tractor undercarriage hummed into life, he became somnambulistically mobile and commenced jerking to and fro, trundling forward, and advancing upon me however involuntarily. Goodwin was not threatening me; on the contrary, he was trying to escape from a resurgent situation.)

Dr. S, in a louder tone of voice but as calmly and steadily as possible in the circumstances: "James Goodwin, the next time you hear me say 'stop,' you will at once disconnect your neural interface and fall peacefully asleep!"

Goodwin, beginning to froth at the mouth and swaying in his frame as his prosthetic lurched forward: "Ach-ach-*arrrggghhh!*"

And finally Dr. S: "STOP!"

Session ends.

X

NO DUFF MSG!
URGENT! URGENT! URGENT!

On this day, 12th Nov 2407, at 2244 Hrs, Cmdr. Abel Berresford, Darkside Luna Base, requests immediate voice contact with Cmdr. Space Central, AZ.

"Abel? This is Frankie Zazarro. What the *hell* is happening up there? Man, I was at Liz's birthday party, and if this is one of your practical…. Are you talking over the *top* of me?"

"Frankie, shut up and listen! I'm really sorry about Liz's party but we have an anomaly. In fact we have five of them. My meteor cannons are locked on them right now and I need to know what to do. I mean, hell, I *know* what to do but SOPs won't let me, not without your say-so."

"An 'anomaly'? Five anomalies? You mean like Anomaly 13?"

"Exactly like that, Frankie! Now let me tell you about it. All nine hundred of us, we're situated in our three interconnected crater domes in a rough triangle of some five acres…but you already know all that; you were the Officer Commanding up here way before me! I'm just putting you in the picture, is all. Anyway, these things appeared out of nowhere maybe twenty or twenty-five minutes ago. They're something like a mile away, in the hills to the north and on the plain in the south, completely encircling the base. And they just sit there like small silver pyramids. They're not doing anything, but their pattern—the way we're surrounded—I mean, this has *got* to be about us! And Frankie, I don't like it at all."

"Abel, General Sellway and my security people are on their way into HQ right now. And meanwhile I'm told we can't get you on screen. Now why the hell is that?"

"Because our comsats are down, that's why."

"Down?"

"Either taken out or blocked in some way. Never mind visuals, you wouldn't be getting voice if not for our surface cable to Earthside! But these things are like sitting ducks, Frankie! And with our cannons…you just say the word and this time we won't simply be firing at chunks of space rock!"

"Abel, listen: you'll do no such thing! Don't even shine a light on those pyramids! You're not the only one with SOPs, you know. Mine are pretty much like yours and while we've been talking I've glanced through them. Know what happened the last time someone flashed a light at one of those things?"

"Yes, I know. Anomaly 13. But I wasn't thinking in terms of flashlights, Frankie. I was thinking in terms of guns that fire so fast and hard they can vaporize incoming meteorites!"

"Abel, hold it a minute. The General is here, and he's been listening in."

"Abel, Gordon Sellway here. When our security people get in we'll look at our options. There's too much history—too much of a situation here—for any one man's decision. Do you copy?"

"*Shit!* I copy, but it looks like one of my gunners doesn't!"

"*What?*"

"Some trigger-happy jerk has just opened up! *Ah! That light…leaping from one pyramid to the next…reaching up like a wall of brilliant white fire, and….* " (Transmission ends.)

XI

"*Ahem!* Voice record of Dr. G. L. Spatzer, at—ummm, let's see—0845 hours on the 13th of November, 2407:

"Just had a call from James Goodwin. He's coming to see me. Puzzling—in fact amazing! Until recently I was the one man he least wanted anything to do with! But bad timing, because right now the HQ is a madhouse—and I don't just mean the psychiatric ward! All of the top brass, the military and their minions, and droves of civil servants rushing to and fro; I daren't step out in the corridor for fear of getting trampled underfoot!

"Understandable in the current circumstances, I suppose. Apparently some idiot paparazzi hack was tuned in on an insecure Earth/Darkside Luna conversation last night and patched it through as an 'exclusive' to his patron news channel…since when it's spread like wildfire!

"This morning it's on the airwaves, the TV screens, and in the papers all over the planet! Two shuttles on course for the moon from UES II, grav-drive *Spirit of Space* inbound from the asteroid belt, and the untried gunship *Sir Galahad* ordered up into Earth orbit. I didn't catch it all: something about 'anomalies'—like Jim Goodwin's, I wonder?—and a total Darkside-Luna shutdown. Space Central working desperately hard, even too hard, to put it about that it's some kind of 'freak power failure' and nothing to be concerned about. Frankly I can't see it. If it's nothing to be concerned about, why is this place in an uproar?

"I can hear Goodwin come purring down the corridor…I'll leave the recorder running. Maybe he'll have something interesting for me. High time, too! I admit I'm beginning to despair of ever getting through to him…."

(The hiss of pneumatic doors opening and the deep-throated purr of a powerful electric motor. Dr. Spatzer's voice warning, "Mind your head, Jim!" And a high-pitched whine quickly fading into silence as the motor shuts down.)

Goodwin's voice: "Surprise, surprise, Doc!"

Dr. S: "Good morning, Jim. You seem in fine spirits!"

Goodwin: "Cheerful, you mean? In a way, I suppose. Not much good feeling down; not any longer, anyway. Fact is I'm ready to talk—about everything. I've remembered everything, Doc—and it's stopped hurting!"

Dr. S, indeed sounding surprised, and perhaps not a little alarmed: "Stopped hurting? But how can that be, Jim? The drugs? I mean even the best painkillers can't—"

Goodwin: "No, it's not my backside, what little is left of it; I'm talking about my head! I can think it through now without it shuts me down every time."

Dr. S: "And you believe you can talk about it? About, well, everything, did you say?"

Goodwin, most eagerly: "That's right. It was the library—the archives, all the restricted stuff that I've been reading—and then to top it off this morning's news. That's what finally did the trick. You see Doc, until now I couldn't figure it out. But now…now I'm pretty sure I know what it was all about."

Dr. S: "The archives? Ah, yes! You've been spending quite a lot of time in the library, haven't you? Your newfound freedom and unrestricted access? We've tried to make everything as easy and as normal as possible for you. Not everyone has that kind of access to the archives. As for this morning's news: do you mean the problem on Darkside?"

Goodwin: "That's what I mean all right—but it isn't just Darkside Base that's got a problem, Doc. No, not at all. So, do you want to hear about it—about everything?"

Dr. S, cautiously: "An unscheduled session, you mean? Right here in my office?"

Goodwin: "Relax, Doc. I'm not going to bite you. That's all over and done with now. Fact is, everything is done with now. I just thought you'd like to know about it before…well before they get here, is all. Then you can make up your mind like I've made up mine."

Dr. S, warily: "But you know, Jim, that's a rather peculiar smile you're wearing. Also…well, you're not making too much sense either. I mean, we've had our little problems, and—"

Goodwin: "I know, and I'm sorry. But I'm okay now, I assure you. And to tell the truth, I don't think there's too much time left. But if you're really not interested, well—"

Dr. S, with a wry chuckle: "Hmmm! So then, maybe you're the *real* psychiatrist here, eh? But okay, I'm hooked, and of course I'll listen to you. So go ahead, explain away. Tell me about…everything."

Goodwin: "It's a long story but I'll cut it short as I can. The reason I wasn't able to do it before was because I couldn't understand how anyone—how any intelligent *thing*, or things—could be so terrifyingly, coldbloodedly, calculatingly merciless. Nothing in my experience, in the skies, on the earth or in the oceans has ever come anywhere near it for what I took to be sheer unfeeling cruelty. But it happened to me, and it happened to poor Sue Rafferty. And it was so horrifically unnatural that my mind was shutting down every time I started to think back on it.

"Okay, let me get started:

"That flash of light from the anomaly had KO'd me, knocked me out cold. Sue too, as it later turned out. So it seems more than likely I dreamed that stuff about looking down on the universe…it's something I'm not sure about. I mean, how could I possibly have done something as weird as that? But one thing *is* for sure: I felt that I'd been moved—conveyed, transported—oh, a very, *very* long way. It was just a feeling I had, that distance was somehow meaningless now….

"Anyway, Sue was awake first.

"I came to when I heard her calling out to me. We were in a couple of purplish-blue bubbles with semi-opaque walls; she was next door, standing with her hands spread on the adjoining wall and looking through at me. The walls distorted things; they had these ripples of blue light moving over them. Whatever was outside our rooms—more of these bubbles, with vague shapes moving around inside them—it all seemed to melt away into a hazy distance. I was on my back, on a flat, circular table with five thin legs. When I stood up I could see a similar table in Sue's bubble. We were both stark naked; our pressure suits and clothing lay in twin heaps against the walls of our respective bubbles, in fact our cells.

"Once I was on my feet, I felt heavy; Earth-heavy, which I wasn't used to. I went toward Sue, touched the wall. It gave a little under my hand but finally resisted me. A force-field of some sort; it had to be. We were naked as babes, as I've said, but in this situation…well hell, that didn't matter at all.

Sue's voice was faint, as if she was in another room—which of course she was—but I know you get my meaning.

"'Jim, where are we?' she said. I could tell she was scared witless. For all that it was warm she stood there shivering but without making a move to cover her parts. Hey, who am I to talk about being scared? I was naked too and I hadn't given a single thought to putting some clothes on. I tried to speak to Sue but when she saw my lips moving she shook her head, said, 'No!' And finally it dawned on me that she wasn't just speaking but shouting at me!

"So I shouted back and she heard me. 'Clothes,' I told her, and I made for my stuff where it was heaped against the wall. I figured that being clothed would at least provide us with something of dignity. But:

"'No!' Sue shouted again as I reached for my drawers.

"And *bang*—I was zapped! There was some kind of isolation field around my clothing. It hummed and sparked, made traceries of fire and knocked me off my feet. *Damn*, that stung! It numbed me from my finger-tips to my armpits! But at least I knew why Sue was naked now, and why I was going to stay that way, too….

"Time passed, quite a bit of time. We got sore throats from shouting at each other, asking pointless questions. And finally we slept…

"When I woke up again, that was when the horror started.

"It was Sue's screams that woke me. And believe me, she was scream-ing! Coming loud and clear even through the bubble walls, it drilled into my nerves, shook me awake and tumbled me off my table bed so that I hit the floor in a heap. And I hobbled over to the wall and looked in on her cell.

"In there with Sue were three of the vague shapes we'd seen before in the bubble rooms outside our own. But they weren't so vague now. As a kid I had been fascinated by all kinds of rocks from fossils to meteorites. It was a sure bet I would be either a paleontologist or a spaceman; and we know how that worked out. But looking at these creatures in Sue's cell, I sudden-ly remembered my favorite fossil, the one I prized over all the others in my small collection: a trilobite some five inches long, nose to tail. Except these things had too many lobes—four in fact—and they were ten feet long; six-feet of it on the deck, held up by God knows how many crab legs, and the front lobe upright, standing four foot tall, with six many-jointed, armlike appendages, three to a side, and swiveling crab eyes on stalks under a chitin cowl. They were as shiny black as my fossil and scurried when they moved, their many legs seeming to flicker, shifting them to, fro, sideways, back-wards, mobile as hell and a lot more nightmarish! Picture clever cock-roach-crabs, with upright, mantis-like front ends—you'll know what I was looking at. But as for what they were doing to Sue…

"Two of them held her pinned down on the table; it's possible they'd come upon her while she was asleep, or I would have heard her screaming before I did. Anyway, they'd put some kind of clamps on her ankles and wrists, an adhesive material, as I later discovered, which stuck to the table and held her fairly motionless. And then…and th-th-then…."

Dr. S, concernedly: "Jim, if you want to stop now…"

Goodwin, after clearing his throat: "No, it's okay. I'll be okay now. Where was I? Oh, yeah:

"So the third member of this trio, he wheeled in a machine. But first he stepped out through the wall, as easy as you like, then returned pushing this machine that floated some six inches off the floor. And by the way, that floor was made of some sort of tough rubber, crisscrossed with thin strips of white metal.

"Anyway, this machine is all glass and silver metal. A very intricate thing…and God, a very devilish one, too! A screen appeared on the joining wall—the wall between Sue's cell and mine—which was just as clear on my side as it must have been on hers. And when these things had positioned this bloody awful machine beside Sue's table, they swung certain of its extensible adjuncts out over her body. One of these was quite obviously some kind of X-ray camera, because a full-size picture of Sue's innards appeared on the screen. Her outline and all of her organs were clearly visible: her heart hammering like mad, stomach heaving, lungs fluttering…she was panting. And yet she kept on screaming, cursing and yelling at these bastards, too, until one of them brought what I figured to be a remote control device over to the wall, looked at the screen, and b-b-began to operate the thing…which operated the machine at Sue's table.

"And on the screen I saw the machine extend a fork-tongued probe of shining silver metal down into poor Sue's mouth! Stabbing through into the back of her neck, it straddled her spinal column and pinned her head to the table. A trickle of blood appeared on the table where twin prongs had poked through the skin at the back of her neck.

"But the terrible thing is, *she was still conscious!* All of Sue's organs were still working: her heart pounding, her bowels churning. If she could have gone on screaming, she'd still have been doing that, too! But as it was it was me—*I* was doing the screaming now—hammering on that soft, impenetrable wall, trying to dig my hands into it, then stepping back and hurling myself at it without doing any good at all; until finally my legs turned to jelly. I flopped to the floor then and just sat there watching the rest of it—unable to drag my eyes away—watching not only the blurred, indefinite activity of the horseshoe-crab aliens at Sue's table but also the hideous *reality* of what they were doing on the crystal-clear wall-screen: her suffering as the roach-like bastard with the remote continued to ogle the screen while proceeding with her t-t-torture!

"And Doc, you can quit your squirming about, and don't even *think* about stopping me! Not one single *fucking* word, you hear? I'll be just fine once I've got all of this shit out of me. And since it's what you've been working at for a couple months now, you should just *sit there and fucking enjoy it*—okay?

"Well, okay then….

"Sue was still jerking about on her table—or her operating table, as I now thought of it—and that wasn't good enough for the aliens, who weren't nearly finished with her. Down came another spindly instrument from the machine: this time a hypodermic of yellow liquid, which stabbed deeply, brutally into her belly. And on the screen I watched the stuff spread through her system.

"Then…she went totally crazy! Her body throbbed, vibrated, went into spasms. God only knows what they'd put into her, but if it was meant to quieten her down…well Christ, surely there were easier ways to knock someone out! Unless they didn't give a damn. And in fact it was as simple as that: they really didn't give a damn! But in the end, as a result of the hellish agony it was causing her, she did go under. And me, when Sue's body went slack, I thanked God—even though I thought she must be dead—still I thanked Him that she wasn't any longer suffering like that. But no, they didn't want her dead, just quiet so they could get on with it. And when I saw how she was still alive, still breathing, and her heart fluttering but no longer threatening to burst, I thanked God again—just for a moment gave thanks—and in the next moment cursed Him! I cursed Him that He was allowing this to happen; cursed God and everything in God's entire fucking universe!

"For now another tool descended on Sue from the machine. A hollow glass drill, it chewed through her skull and passed maybe a quarter-inch into the front of her brain, where it paused to vacuum up some clear liquid and a little grey tissue; which was when I threw up.

"But for all that I was sick I just couldn't turn away; it was like I was hypnotized; I simply *had to know*! And I saw them take samples of Sue's liver, her kidneys and lungs, even marrow from her bones; but never enough to kill her, not yet. And each time the machine bit into her, its tools would burn bright with some weird energy, cauterizing the wound. And my teeth were beginning to hurt, aching from the way I was grinding them. And I reckon it's that, Doc—what they did to Sue and would later do to

me—that brought on my problem with needles and sharp instruments. Can you b-blame me? Well *can* you, eh?

"But you know, as bad as I felt about Sue I was more scared for myself. I mean, she had been the first, but when would they start on me? What does that make me, some kind of lousy coward? Well let me tell you, Doc, while there isn't a man in the world I would ever run away from, there isn't *anyone* on *any* world who wouldn't want to escape from the horror of the notion that he'd be next under *that* machine on one of *those* t-tables!

"Anyway, let me get on….

"Finally, dissolving Sue's clamps, the bugs turned off the wall-screen, took their God-awful machine and samples and left. With the screen gone there was no way to know if Sue was living or dead. And then, mentally and physically exhausted—because Sue and me, we hadn't had a bite to eat nor even a sip of water since we were taken—I fell asleep again…but on the floor and against the wall, *not* on my table! And though I nightmared, still I somehow managed to sleep—

"—Until I sensed movement and started awake!

"One of the bugs was just leaving, passing out through the wall as if it was mist. There was a bowl of pale blue liquid on the table, along with a carrot-like root with purple skin and a tuft of blue-green leaves. I took the smallest sip of the liquid and it was…well, water! The tuber had a bitter taste but it stayed down. After finishing off the tuber and drinking some of the water I went to look through the wall into Sue's bubble. She just lay on her table, completely motionless. And still not knowing if she was alive or dead—full to the brim with horror and despair—once again I dropped off to sleep—

"—And again sensed movement!

"It was Sue, staggering here and there as she made her way over to the wall. I could scarcely believe she was on her feet! But as she reached the wall she just slid down it, went to her knees with her pale face and one shoulder leaning against it.

"'Jim, they…they….' Her voice was so weak and gasping, I had to put my ear to the wall in order to hear it. 'They *hurt* me, Jim.'

"'I know,' I told her. 'I saw it all. Oh God, I'm so sorry, kid! But look over there, on the floor there. The water is safe and that carrot thing is edible. You have to eat; you've got to survive, got to keep going, Sue.' That's what I told her, but I really don't know why. It was bullshit, that's all.

"She crawled away, went and ate, then curled herself into a small round ball under her table and went to sleep. And despite that I repeatedly told myself to stay awake and keep watch over her, finally I too fell asleep again. Maybe it was something in the water they'd given us, some kind of drug. But so what? Even if I had stayed awake, what then? I wasn't able to help myself, let alone Sue....

"...There was movement! Starting awake, I saw that the b-b-bugs were back in Sue's bubble room again. So was their torture machine, and the screen was back up on the wall. Oh, God! Oh my good God! I shouldn't have cursed Him so! Because...because—

"—Because I could see it was going to be the same all over again—but I could *never* have foreseen that it was going to be even worse!

"The alien operating the remote was ogling the screen with his knobby crab eyes, and the hellish machine was letting down a vibrating tool toward Sue where she was clamped to her table. Awake, aware, she was much too weak to struggle or even scream, but it didn't stop her from trying. Very faintly, I could hear the croaking sounds she made, the gurgling when her mouth dribbled foam and her panting blew bubbles in it.

"They hadn't needed to nail her head down this time, so she was able to turn it, her eyes bulging as she watched the vibrating tool descending toward her shoulder. It was a cutting instrument of some kind, its sharp edge an almost invisible blur as it came down on her right arm an inch below where it joined her shoulder. And *zzzzztttt,* it was through her arm—I mean *right* through it—before the blood could even begin to spurt! But I saw the look on Sue's face, the way her eyes popped out further yet, and knew that she couldn't believe it any more than I did. It *had* to be a nightmare!

"Then the blood spurted, and we both knew it wasn't a nightmare. And as they cauterized her stump Sue passed out, but this time I didn't thank God because I'd tried it once and it hadn't worked. And while I had no idea what would happen next, still I was pretty sure I wouldn't be able to bear it.

"And I was right.

"By then I'd lost my voice...you yell and scream for long enough, loud enough, and that happens. And there I was kneeling at the wall, sobbing like a little kid, watching as they turned Sue face down and cut her again: her entire left leg this time, buttock and all right down to the gleaming pink bones. From the hip at the top to the coccyx at the bottom, then up round Sue's bush and back to the hip, they'd cut her. And at a stroke—or more properly at a slice and a bloody scoop, but in any case as quickly as that—what had been beautiful was hideously ugly.

"Once again they cauterized that crimson flood; and on the wall-screen before they switched it off and left with her amputated limbs, I saw but could scarcely believe that even now her heart was beating, however unevenly. And I know that you'll forgive me, Doc, if I tell you that by then I was wishing it would stop. I wanted it done with—wanted her dead—because I knew that Sue would want it, too....

"Time passed...

"I have some vague recollections of partial consciousness, of being awake again, if only for a hazy moment or two, and of seeing renewed roach activity in Sue's bubble. But as for what was happening in there: this time I couldn't watch. I couldn't *bear* to; I convinced myself that it was all a bad dream that I could simply turn away from, and lapsed into a period of delirious praying, raving, cursing and what have you.

"Just as well, I suppose, because when I came out of it and looked at her—and was actually able to *understand* what I was looking at—I saw that they'd taken her other leg, too. There was only half a woman on that table now. But...what the hell? They'd *returned* Sue's arm! Limp and white as a piece of marble, it was just lying there beside her trunk, along with some other bits and pieces that I believed I recognized as the s-s-samples that they'd taken earlier.

"It was all there on the table in Sue's bubble room: everything that had been a beautiful girl; well, except her legs and butt. And nothing of beauty left any more, only a lifeless grey mutilated trunk with slack breasts, a dead face and glazed fish eyes. But at least she was dead now, and I was able to speak to God again and thank him sincerely this time.

"Oddly enough, I was able to laugh a little, too. In fact I laughed quite a lot. I laughed so hard it hurt my ribs and then I knew I had to stop. So what do you reckon, Doc? I was maybe a little crazy? Maybe even now, just a touch crazy? But it's okay, Doc, it's okay. In fact my state of mind is the very last thing you need to worry about, because I can see everything perfectly clearly now....

"So where was I? Oh yes:

"And then...and then—

"—Finally they came for me, and it was my t-t-turn."

Dr. S, urgently: "Jim, we...well we sort of know the rest of it, don't we? So if you want to stop now—"

Goodwin, his voice grating: "No, you *don't* know the rest of it. No, I *don't* want to stop now! I want you to know everything about these fucking monsters so you'll finally know what's coming! And it's not just them who are the monsters; we've been the monsters, too. But that was in our time—when we were the dominant species—and now it's their time. I want you to understand how it works, that's all, want you to make the connection on your own if you haven't already done so. The fish fights the hook, Doc. The tree fern hurls its javelins, and even the lowly bramble has its thorns."

Dr. S, baffled: "Fish? Brambles? Tree ferns? Fighting?"

Goodwin, as if uninterrupted: "Well, and so did I: I fought back. But when it comes down to survival, when it's the hunter-gatherer—whether he's a man-like ape with a club or an alien with superior technology— when it's him against whatever else is out there and he's hungry...then it's always the dominant, more advanced guy who wins. Don't you see that?"

Dr. S, very concerned now: "Jim, you're not making too much sense. And I really *do* know the rest of it. Those terrible creatures were experimenting on you, seeing just how much it would take to kill you. Why, just looking at you I can see...I mean it's pretty obvious...God, I didn't mean to say *any* of that!"

Goodwin, cutting in, quite obviously abstracted but calmer now: "Oh yes, I fought back. They weren't going to slice up my kidneys, my liver and brain—weren't going to suck out my bone marrow and cut off my arms— not without a fight, they weren't! But as it worked out those things weren't what they were after. They'd found what they'd been looking for in Sue; they weren't any longer interested in what they'd already rejected, only in what they'd kept and what I had still got.

"And now it was my turn, and they came for me: the three of them, their torture machine, their wall screen monitor and all. But I was waiting for them.

"The first one in—the moment he came skittering through that wall—I was up off the floor, launching myself at him. I hadn't been drinking their drugged water; I was weak and dehydrated, but I was desperate too and full of fury! That first one in, I grabbed at his most vulnerable parts: his slimy, swiveling eyes-stalks under their blue chitin cowl. And how I yanked on them, hauling on them just as hard as I could!

"And oh, I hurt him—did I ever *hurt* the bastard! Stinking blue goo spurted from the sockets where I'd almost wrenched his stalks out, and all the while he was hissing and whistling like steam from a pressure cooker. Damn, but I really hurt that ugly fuck! Oh, yes. Yes I did...

"And then he and his pals hurt me.

"Cattle prods? I thank God I never worked on a ranch in the days before we synthesized beef! And as for tasers: you think I could be a cop and use one of those things? Not likely, not any more...not even if I had my legs...and not even if we stood a chance of winning this one. Because now I know what 'hurting' means.

"I suffered, Doc. I mean I really suffered. They shocked me and shocked me, needled me and needled me. They didn't need to, because I was down on the floor, writhing around in agony after the first prod. But they did it anyway, because I'd hurt one of theirs. So in a way I suppose they're pretty much like us: they don't turn the other cheek. Or if they do, it's only to cut and cauterize, ha-fucking-ha!"

Dr. S, consolingly yet very nervously: "Oh, Jim...Jim...Jim!"

Goodwin, his motorized adjunct whining into life, the sound of his tractor in motion: "So you see, Doc, you knew the *how* of it and the *what* of it, but you didn't know the *why*. And to tell the truth neither did I till I got mobile again and was able to visit the restricted archives and read the documents we rescued from the wreck of the *Starspike Explorer*. I had friends on that ship or I wouldn't have bothered, wouldn't have been interested. But as it works out...well the way I see it, what was written in those documents was very relevant. In fact it explained just about everything that I've been trying to explain to you."

Dr. S, warningly: "Don't get too close to that window, Jim! You're doing great with those controls but you haven't got them down pat just yet and we're nine stories high up here!"

Goodwin: "I just want to look out, that's all. Look out on what I used to look down on from the shuttles and UES IV. Used to, yes, but look at me now. Earthbound—stone cold sober and yet 'legless,' ha-fucking-ha!— nine stories up at Space Central HQ, looking out over the entire complex. I can't see nearly as far as I used to, Doc, not even from up here, but since reading those *Starspike Explorer* documents I sure understand a hell of a lot more! Have you read that stuff, Doc?"

Dr. S: "Why, yes, as a matter of fact. The investigation is ongoing and has been for a long time, but I was called in from the beginning to do a psychological study, a posthumous assessment of...of—"

Goodwin: "—Of a certain female crew member? Namely Laurilu Nagula? Oh, I can understand that well enough. But can't you see the relevance, I mean aside from just the psychology? Can't you see the parallels, the analogy?"

Dr. S, wonderingly: "Parallels? Analogy?"

Goodwin, thoughtfully: "Well, maybe not. Because it doesn't—or didn't—apply to you. But it certainly applies to me. I think that if you can find the time, assuming we're to be given *enough* time, maybe you should read those papers again, Doc. And especially Laurilu's concerns about all the waste, how much she hated it." (Goodwin's laughter.) "Well, me too, Laurilu! But on a far more personal level, right?"

Dr. S: "Jim, I—"

Goodwin: "Read what she wrote, and what she said to Michael Gilchrist, the ship's so-called 'exobioecologist,' that time in her bunk; what she said about the shark fishermen. And not only that but what *he* said about them: how they threw back what they didn't want, just tossed them back alive or dead, back into, or maybe I should say *onto*—"

Dr. S, faintly: "Back onto the…the…*oh my God!*"

Goodwin: "Now you're getting it! Now you're seeing it, Doc! It's our position in the universal food chain, that's all. What a tree fern is to us—"

Dr. S: "—We are to…to…?"

Goodwin: "Exactly! Except with us there's this problem with the waste, that's all. Makes you wonder what the French do with all those soft little bodies, now doesn't it?"

Dr. S, weakly, wonderingly: "The French?"

Goodwin: "Sure. I mean, they know the parts that suit their taste buds, but what do they do with the bits that don't, eh?"

Dr. S: "The bits that don't? You mean the rest of the f-f-f—*for God's sake!*"

Goodwin: "Just one more thing before I go, Doc. How many of these prosthetics is the Corps working on? I mean apart from my new, light-weight model—which I'm sure I won't be needing."

Dr. S, dazedly: "How m-many?"

Goodwin, revving his motor: "Because if you want my advice, Doc, I reckon you need to be building those things on an automated production line or lines, and that you should get them up and running just as soon as possible."

Dr. S: "Jim, what are you saying? What are you d-doing?"

Goodwin: "Goodbye, Doc. It's me for the compost heap, while there's still some room on it."

(The sound of his tractor's motor revving more yet, then of grinding gears, glass shattering, torn metal, and moments later a jarring near-distant crash.) And finally:

Dr. S, his sobbing voice repeating over and over again: "Oh Jesus! Oh my God! Oh Jesus! Oh my G-g-god…!"

XII

FEASIBILITY REPORT

Sol III Equivalents, Haquar Standard:

Diameter...............1.215 approx.
Day.............0.922 approx.

Mass...............1.163 approx.
Atmos.................Acceptable, if a little high in nitrogen, which will be of small consequence once our automated farms and domed processing units are established.
Life:—
A surprising diversity of flora and fauna! The higher or "dominant" lifeforms are bipedal; indeed, their pedal extremities are a delicacy and highly recommended. A shame that the flavor and texture of their vital organs should be unappetizing to Haquarian tastes and even somewhat toxic in concentrated chemical and bacterial content; a great waste. Likewise the trunk, head, and stringy upper appendages: too bony, messy, time-consuming; generally unsatisfactory.

There has been among my team some facetious conjecture that perhaps these creatures have passed too far along the multiversal evolutionary path to be considered mere pabulum, provender, or gourmet pap. Such speculation was put to the test, as usual, by measuring the species' progress against that of the Haquari.

They have two sexes: an utterly inefficient means of reproduction. Even the most primitive, amoeban lifeforms are capable of fission. Having no telepathic capability, no hive awareness, no Oneness, their principal means of communication is by sounds produced by the expulsion of gases from their mouths; while for mass communication they rely on a system of ponderous electronic transmissions.

With regard to evolution, this species would appear to have reached its peak. In exploration—having no concept of Dimensional Instantaneity—it can never conceivably occupy anything larger than a tiny niche in one small corner of what it unimaginatively perceives as the universe…in other words a single space-time plane of existence with no parallels except in semi-metaphysical theory! As for the IQ of the species: compared with an average Haquari intelligence quotient set at 10, the human score would be 0.0025 approximately. Therefore my assessment—based not only on the degree of Haquari necessity but principally on multiversal levels of progress, intelligence, and achievement—is that this species may only be placed in the 'non-sentient livestock' category.

END NOTE:—

With a population in excess of eight billion, Sol III has to be recognized as a major Haquari food source. Automated farming is not only feasible but practical, and in the light of the accelerating decline in sustainable home world resources, I recommend this world's immediate exploitation. Under modern, managed farming procedures—processing bone as fertilizer and undesirable protein as provender for the livestock, etc.—we should enjoy at least two hundred years usage before the source of this par-ticularly nutritious comestible is exhausted....

This Being the Pronouncement of Ak'n N'Ghar XXVII,
Exobioecologist of Haquar Prime, 2731st Parallel,
on the 7138th Day of the 2nd Haquari Billennium.

★ ·★· ★

Gaddy's Gloves

This next one was written in the summer of 1988 and appeared in the pamphlet-cum-program book of the World Fantasy Convention when the traveling con came to London in 1991. Since the pamphlet was distributed to attendees only and "Gaddy's Gloves" wasn't reprinted, this is virtually an "unknown" Lumley. And of course its "science" element is now dated by virtue of all the incredible advances in communication technology, computer gaming, and like that. In fact, and if memory serves, even back in 1991 the kids were playing some pretty fantastic arcade games! Ah, but there was never a player like Gunner Gaddy....

I

DOWN IN THE CARGO hold, Grint Pavanaz let himself out of his crate, ate a sandwich and hooked up his 'Vader to the nearest power point. An hour later and halfway through his tenth game, a hatch clanged open and crewmen came clattering with blasters drawn and primed. And they dragged him in front of Captain Cullis. The Captain—bald, fat, red-faced—was more than somewhat peeved and threatened to turn Pavanaz into flotsam. "What if we'd stowed that crate in vacuum?" he snapped through his gash of a mouth.

"You couldn't." Pavanaz shrugged. "I paid seven creds for that air-storage sticker."

"Oh?" Cullis snorted. "And every air-storage sticker gets stored in air, right? Let me tell you something, Puffernuts: sometimes we vacuum *all* of our crates to kill off the roaches! Especially coming off a swamp like Gizzich IV. And sometimes we irradiate 'em too, and decon before delivery!"

Pavanaz was unrepentant; he shrugged again and said: "Wow!" but very dryly. "You irradiate seeds, yeah? And you vacuum temperate atmosphere tools? Well no wonder your freighters have a better than fifty percent 'damaged in transit' record!"

"Twenty-two percent on this ship, Puffernuts!" The Captain was touchy. "Or twenty-two point zero one if we jettison you!"

"Naw." Pavanaz picked his nose. "See, I dropped a line to Earth to let people know I was coming—and aboard which scow. Also, I researched this bucket. I discovered you run a tight ship, Captain—so no more horror stories about spacing your passengers and such. Hell, you run *such* a tight ship you even monitor internal power drain! It's how you found me: the juice my 'Vader was burning."

"Your what?" the Captain scowled. And Pavanaz explained.

When he was through they went back down to storage and examined his machine. Pavanaz glowed. "She was the latest thing in Ozzie's Arcade back on Gizzich IV. But at a centricred a shot you could go broke getting yourself a decent score. So I entered Ozzie's place kind of late one night and sort of, well, rearranged the wiring. Fixing these things was my job, see—or in this case, unfixing them. So Ozzie sent for me the next day and I checked her out, and told him: "No way—she's a goner—computer's cracked." He sold her to me for scrap.

"I put her right, added a few tricks, played till my fingers went flat. It took time, but now I'm the best there is."

What Pavanaz didn't say was that Ozzie had called round his place a week later and found him playing the machine. He'd flared up, likewise Pavanaz; somehow the latter's razor-edged knife had contrived to cut the Arcade King's throat. Living at the edge of one of Gizzich IV's biggest swamps, it was no big deal. Ozzie had gone down slow but sure in a mile of mud.

The odds against anyone tagging Grint Pavanaz as a killer were in the seven figures bracket, but he'd panicked anyway. He stole a little money, crated the machine, paid for its passage to Earth, then climbed in the crate with the 'Vader....

The 1st Mate snapped his fingers. "The Game Show!" he said. "The big TV tournament, coming in three months' time. While they watch, twenty-five billion kids match their skills alongside the best in the Federation."

Pavanaz grinned, blew on his fingernails and polished them on his shirt.

"Is that what this is about?" said the Captain. "You stowed away to Earth to play games?"

"October, 2482," said Pavanaz. "Eliminations for a month, the quarter- and semi-finals played off on the 29th, finally the Big Game on the 30th. I shall be there, gentlemen…you are looking at the new champion. A million creds in it, a half-million for the runner-up, and a quarter-million for—"

"We get the picture," the Captain cut him short. "So you're that good, eh? Care to show us?"

"Sure," said Pavanaz. "Want to make a small wager?"

Pavanaz was a skinny twenty-one-year-old. Less meat than a mantis, short-cropped black hair that wouldn't fall into his eyes when he played, fingers like a pianist, and a razor-honed mind. And a slant to his mouth that told of a special sort of cynicism. A brilliant kid, thought the Captain. Most kids were these days, but all wasted. In all the entire list of charted, settled systems there wasn't enough real work to go round. Oh, plenty of farming out on the new frontiers, lots of dirty fingernail jobs, but nothing for one like Pavanaz. Except one chance in a million that he'd make a million and retire to one of the resort worlds. Cullis was more or less right, that was all Pavanaz wanted: a million credits, a beach and the latest model 'Vader. The problem was, he didn't care how he got them. Cullis did care, but he was saving it for later.

Pavanaz climbed into the bouncing, swiveling bucket-seat of his machine and sat there with his eyes closed for a couple of seconds. 'Vaders had been around for five hundred years and more. At first they were expensive toys, then trainers for pilots on Mother Earth, finally trainers for pilots off the Earth. For when men moved out into space and found the Khuum waiting, the 'Vaders had been given a new lease on life; but updated, faster, full of tricks that the kids of the late 20th Century never even dreamed of. Trainers, yes—for the guys who lived through, died in, and at last won the Khuum wars. Since when, what with virtual reality and all, they'd evolved, and evolved, and....

"You gone to sleep, kid?" said the Captain. Pavanaz opened his eyes, switched her on, and showed them who was asleep. They didn't have the con, but they could look round him and cop some of the excitement. And his game was exciting, indeed inspired, a virtuoso performance. Wraparound 3D made it as close to real as possible, and Pavanaz played it that way: no longer a skinny kid but a fighter pilot out among the stars, on patrol, searching for the enemy.

Out there in deep space his hands, eyes and brain were like parts of the computer he controlled, or half-controlled. No one ever "won" one of these games; the machine won; the idea was to last longer than anyone else and rack up a higher score. For no matter how many of the enemy you destroyed, the computer would conjure up bigger, faster, more powerful Khuum ships. The big ones carried the highest score, but before you could reach *them* you had to kill off all the small-fry who were trying hard to kill you! So in fact you played yourself, because your skill governed the strength of your opponent: the harder you fought, the greater the machine's efforts against you.

A fleet of Khuum was out there; they spotted Pavanaz and began to pivot; he was into and through them, killing them off fore and aft, port and starboard. They were no match for him. He looked for bigger fish and found sharks! Behind the scattering fleet, a dozen highly conjectural vessels with all the regular Khuum tricks and then some, turned their needle snouts on him. Pavanaz launched into them, zigzagged to avoid their beams, set his bucket-seat fishtailing. Strapped in, he somehow ignored the motion to concentrate on the game in hand.

At first surprised, the aliens burst asunder, blew up in mad blasts of light and sound which were real enough to add to the reality, quickly threw up their shields. Pavanaz discharged shield-scramblers, following up with Takka Beams that homed on the scramblers, like iron filings to a magnet. And once through the disrupted alien screens, then they homed in on the ships. Pavanaz sliced through debris aware that the Khuum had regrouped and were hot on his littered trail.

His score mounted on the monitor; he dripped sweat till his clothes stuck to him; his hands moved like crazed spiders over the controls. The din of exploding ships was deafening as their beams crept ever closer. Pavanaz's score went up and the computer compensated. A Khuum battle-cruiser swam into view, and behind it a carrier launching mines and missiles. Pavanaz tripped into hyperspace, burned the cruiser with his exhaust, threw all power to his screens and deflected the carrier's hypermissiles. He tripped back into normal space and found his screen full of heavy metal! The carrier was dead ahead! No one had *ever* taken out a carrier before!

Pavanaz hit all of his firing buttons simultaneously and chewed a passage right through the carrier's belly. All around him, white and yellow light blazed like the heart of hell; his earphones were full of the scream of metal warping out of existence; disintegrating debris blinded him…so that he didn't even see the whirling, buckled girder that smashed his cockpit and ended the game….

His bucket-seat stopped gyrating; Pavanaz hung limp, drenched over the controls; the scoreboard was alive with flashing lights, and his score was 4,202,786.

"Phew!" said the 1st Mate. "Here, let me try."

"You?" Pavanaz got down, steadied himself against a bulkhead. "You have hands like…like plates of meat!"

"Kid," the 1st Mate glowered, "I was doing it for real when you were navigating a hole in your Ma's tights!" He got aboard, switched on, lasted seventeen point three seconds before being blown to hell. His score was 21,002. Which didn't say much for his war stories. The others didn't do nearly so well, and Captain Cullis got the lowest score of all. Pavanaz sniggered somewhat, which wasn't a good move.

"Pav," said the Captain, "I think you could win."

"Tell me about it," said Pavanaz.

"But you won't, 'cos you're not going to Earth. Not on my 'scow,' anyway."

Pavanaz looked uneasy, said, "You don't scare me, Captain. I checked you out. You've made a round trip, visited a dozen worlds, picked up cargoes all destined for Earth. Your ETA is end of August, which gives me a month to enter the competition and catch up on current innovations. So…you must mean you'll hand me over, charge me with being a stowaway. And you know what next? It will take at least three months to bring me to trial, and by then I'll be the champion. Runner-up at worst. All the worlds love a winner, and you can buy an awful lot of freedom with half a million creds!"

"That's your other big problem," Captain Cullis told him. "Next to being full of shit, you don't listen too good. Let's try it again. I said: you're–not–going–to–Earth."

Pavanaz's upper lip twitched. "I don't follow you."

"Exactly: you won't follow me. Not from Shankov's World!"

Shankov's World, reputed to be one of the wettest planets in the Federation! It lay close by, along the route home. Pavanaz licked suddenly dry lips, shook his head, said, "Eh? But you're fully loaded. Your manifesto doesn't say anything about picking stuff up on Shankov's World."

"Who mentioned cargo?" The 1st Mate was all wide-eyed innocence.

Pavanaz glanced slack-jawed at him, then back at the Captain who told him: "You may know your fighters and your Khuum, and all the rest of the computer-generated junk in there." He sneered at the invader. "But you're not too hot on these big haulers, are you." It was a statement not a question.

"Shankov's?" Pavanaz shook his head again, a little desperately now. "Why would you want to put me down on…" The truth hit him like a thunderbolt. "Fuel!"

The 1st Mate nodded. "Show us a computer that can generate that stuff, you won't need to play in the games tournament!"

"Meanwhile." The captain grinned. "We're just a day out from Shankov's—and you're in the brig!" As Pavanaz was led stumbling away, he added: "And kid—I hope you like rain…."

II

Pavanaz didn't like rain.

Shankov's World was nine-tenths water. Its sun spent its time sucking water up from one half of the planet and dumping it on the other. When it wasn't raining it was misty, and vice versa. The other thing Shankov's World had lots of was lowlife. And fish. Drop a bent pin in the water on Shankov's, you'd pull out a fish. Put a small piece of something edible on the hook, the water would boil!

Because the living was easy, Shankov's attracted bums and riffraff. The rich riffraff had greenhouses with solariums and swimming pools and rarely came out, and the bums lived how they could. The young of both sets frequented the area in the vicinity of the spaceport, where "the action" was, and a good many of them played 'Vaders. Pavanaz wasn't through yet. There were kids here with creds, and his face wasn't known like back on Gizzich IV. Customs passed him as Human; he paid Visitor's Tax and a returnable import fee on his 'Vader, borrowed a fork-lift to carry the machine out of the spaceport to the doors of the nearest arcade: "Fat Bill's Place." Oh, Shankov's was real class!

Fat Bill was a blob about sixty-two inches in all directions; he wheezed as Pavanaz and a handful of splashers-by half-dragged, half-carried the 'Vader into an empty corner in the arcade's front hall. And he waited patiently while Pavanaz used the edges of his hands to squeegee the water out of his shirt and pants. It was "summer" and the rain was warm.

"I'm Bill," he wheezed when Pav was done. "You should buy yourself a plastimac, Mac."

"I'm Grint Pavanaz," said Pavanaz. "And I will."

"S'funny," said Fat Bill, scratching his head. "I don't recall ordering this baby."

"You didn't," Pavanaz informed. "She's mine."

Fat Bill narrowed his eyes a little. "In my arcade?"

"Just until I can catch a ship out of here," said Pavanaz.

Fat Bill's eyes narrowed more yet. "See," he said, "I don't see much in that for me. I mean, there's a warehouse next door where you can stable this beast. So why clutter up my place, eh?"

"I can explain," said Pavanaz.

"Make it good," Fat Bill told him "and fast, before this 'Vader of yours gets headed for one big oxidization problem." He inclined his head towards the door.

Pavanaz stripped the plastic off his machine in front of a mainly disinterested crowd. They pulled faces at it and moved away. Nothing new here. Pav looked at Fat Bill. "I can pay you three creds a day just to keep her here." Fat Bill nodded. "That might be OK—except I like the kids to play *my* machines, you know? It's my living."

"That's good," Pavanaz agreed, forking out three credits. "No one plays this one but me. I've got the key." He checked there was no one within earshot. "Listen, this could be good for both of us."

Fat Bill stepped closer. "Keep talking," he said.

Pavanaz took out a square of soft cloth with a trace of machine oil, commenced wiping down the 'Vader, removing every last trace of moisture. "See," he said, "nobody—but *nobody*—plays these things like I do. So…I wager my game against your top scorers. I bet my money against theirs. And I give 'em good odds. When they lose, we split sixty-forty on each days' take."

"You're short on shekel, right?"

"I need a stake to get to Earth, that's all."

"And you're better than the kids who come in here?"

"Better believe it."

"Look—Pasternak?—maybe you haven't noticed, but Shankov's World is wet. No outdoor sports here, 'cept fishing. The kids round here; they're *experts*. You never seen such players!"

"Except on the Games Shows," said Pavanaz.

"Ah!" The other's piggy eyes opened wide. "So that's it!" He laughed out loud, finished up coughing. Bill's condition and Shankov's climate didn't work. "Don't kill me," he said. "Every kid who ever thought he could play is putting his mother on the streets to buy a ticket to Earth. What makes you so special?"

Pavanaz scowled. "OK, I'll show you. Do you have anyone in here right now who can actually play these things?"

Fat Bill looked at him sideways. "In the back," he finally said. "The 'Vaders are in the back. On Shankov's we keep as far out of the rain as possible. Centricred machines out front, big stuff in the back. You want players? I'll show you players."

Pavanaz followed him into the arcade, through opaque glass humidity doors. And Fat Bill showed him the players.

Pav watched awhile. A couple of the kids were OK, that's all. Gizzich had guys who could eat the best of these, and Pavanaz had eaten *all* of them! He told Fat Bill: "Bear with me," and yelled, "Five gets you fifteen I'm the best there is!"

A crewcut runt who looked much like Pavanaz (except his expression was mainly innocent), turned from the game he was watching and glanced at Pav. The player, the runt, and a crowd of local kids that had been watching cursed loud and vicious as he was blown to bits by the Khuum. He leapt out of the bucket and tore through the spectators, intent on Pavanaz's throat.

"Was that you yelling?" he snarled, his face purple. "You put me off, ruined my game, you sonofa—"

"Hold it, Kem," said the one with the crewcut, getting between them. He was fast and moved like silk, and Pavanaz recognized someone who would be a good player. Also someone with authority—among the 'Vader-addicts, anyway.

"*What?*" Kem was outraged. He was twice as big as the runt but held back. "Aces, this guy cost me a big score! For no good reason he comes in here mouthing off, I'm distracted, and—"

"I saw all that," said Aces. "Also that you were about to be blown sky-high. So he put you off a little—maybe. So what? Didn't you hear what the man said? He said five gets you fifteen he's the best."

Kem looked past Aces at Pavanaz. "Shit," he said, "this beanpole doesn't look like he ever *had* fifteen!"

Pavanaz waved a wad at them. "I have it," he said; "and a lot more. But I'm greedy and you suckers are in here spending money that could be mine. So can you play or can't you? I mean, if you don't want to try me out—hell, there are other arcades where I won't be wasting my talent!" He offered them his best come-and-get-it sneer, and began to turn away. But Aces caught his sleeve and stopped him.

Pavanaz looked at the hand on his arm until it was taken away, then said: "Yeah?"

"Kem could probably take you," said Aces, all soft-voiced. "And if he can't, I sure as hell can."

So you're the big cat around here, are you? But out loud Pav said, "Zat right, Kem? You play good? You can borrow five to go after my fifteen?"

"I don't borrow *shit!*" Kem slapped a five into Aces' open hand. Aces held out his hand to Pav, who stuck three fives in it. "What's your name, anyway, beanpole?" Kem scowled. "I like to know whose money I'm spending."

"Name's Grint Pavanaz," said Pav, "but you can call me The Man." Kem's score was still lit up on the 'Vader screen. Nine hundred and eighty-seven thousand was OK—but only just. Pavanaz knew he could beat it without even trying, but he wouldn't.

"Checking my score?" Kem grinned. "Starting to feel warm?" But then he snarled again: "Remember, it would have been a lot higher if you hadn't bust in here mouthing off!"

"That was when you were playing for laughs," Pav told him. "Anybody can make a score when there's nothing riding. But now it's for money, which is different." He bowed sarcastically and offered Kem the bucket-seat. "You want to show me what you're made of?"

"Brother—Pfefferminz?—do *you* have things to learn!" Kem grinned and climbed into the bucket, paid for the game, scored almost one and a quarter million before being scrambled. But he was an amateur like the rest of them. They didn't live it, that was their trouble. And this time Pav wouldn't either.

He got into the seat, let her roll and was taken out with a score of seven hundred and sixty thousand. Kem was jubilant. He laughed at Pav and yelled, "Hey, you got any more of the green stuff you want to give away?"

The crowd hee-heed and hoo-hooed. Pav scowled. "So you were lucky. Hell, it was the first time I played this model!"

"Excuses, excuses!" Kem snorted, laughing nasally.

Pavanaz scowled harder, yanked out his wad. "Laughing boy," he said, "I got eighty-seven here, all I'm holding. My eight-seven against yours—or is that too rich for you?"

Aces stood to one side, arms folded on his chest. Not as innocent as he looked, he believed he'd seen all this before. Heard about it, anyway. His eyes narrowed where they followed Pav's every move. Kem, on the other hand: he obviously wasn't thinking straight—or maybe he was bloated with success.

Eighty-seven creds! Kem's mouth formed a silent "O." He counted thirty-one out of his pocket, plus the twenty Aces was holding. "Fifty-one," he said, biting his lip. "I'm looking for thirty-six more. Anyone want to double his money, fast?"

"I'm with you, Kem!" A shriveled kid with specs pushed his way forward. He counted out thirty-six into Kem's sweaty paw.

Which was when Aces cut in. "You sure you want to do this?"

Kem grinned. "Are you kidding? This is candy!"

"I'd say it was hard shekel," Aces retorted. "But—" and he shrugged, "—it's your ass."

Kem still couldn't see it. "Hell, no! It's *his* ass, Aces!"

The opponents handed over their cash to Fat Bill, who just happened to be standing there. And Pav told Kem: "Your turn in the hot seat, I believe?"

Kem clocked a million six hundred and forty-nine thousand nine hundred and ninety-one—and Pav took it exactly *nine* higher to a million six hundred and fifty thousand. This time Kem had sweated, but Pav wasn't even mildly fazed.

As he got down from the bucket Kem looked at his score, shook his head, and staggered away through the crowd to throw up in a corner. Fat Bill stood them with his bottom jaw flapping and the money flapping in his hand—until Pavanaz snatched it from him. And: "That's all, folks," Pav grinned.

"Not so fast, hotshot," said Aces, having moved in close. "You knew you could beat him. It was robbery."

"Now you're *really* joking," Pav sneered. "Is it illegal to bet on a sure thing? Or are you saying he was the best you have to offer, and you don't much cotton to a new champ? Sure it was robbery. Like he said: candy from a baby! So unless the rest of you kids have business with me, I'll just—"

"My turn," Aces cut in. "I can't fly as high as you, Paraquat, but I've got fifty—if you'd care to go for it…?"

Pavanaz looking like he might accept, narrowed his eyes, then said: "Naw, who needs it?"

"You're backing off? Backing down?" Aces' face was blank.

Pavanaz shook his head. "Lessons from me are expensive," he said. "Fifty—" he shrugged "who needs it?"

Aces nodded sourly. "You played Kem when all he had was five. What's wrong, Paraquat? Nerve gone?"

"I'd seen Kem's game." Pav grinned. "He looked easy to me." His words sounded loose but he'd chosen them with care.

"You only play the easy ones?" Aces spoke quietly but *his* words held a sneer. The sort that said: brother, you are real *chickenshit*! The crowd held its breath.

Pavanaz made himself go white. He'd had the practice; it wasn't hard. "Find another twenty-five—make it seventy-five—" he snapped, "you've got yourself a game!"

The rest of the gang forked out and again the stake went to Fat Bill. And Bill was grinning now. He liked Pavanaz a lot.

Five minutes later it was all over; Pavanaz had a pocketful of creds; the kids followed him as he went back out through the humidity doors to his 'Vader. When they got there he turned and said: "Listen, chumps. This one is mine and it makes those antiques in back look like so much scrap. But this is a nasty big old planet for nice expensive metal like this, which is why the Fat Man is going to find me a nice dry room all my own to keep her in.

If you guys are good, I might let you watch me practice with this baby. And if you're *especially* good—you could even get to play a game or two yourselves! So tell me, am I good to you or am I good to you."

"Shaganass," said Aces, now recovered. "I just can't hate someone who plays like you do. But I can't admire you either. So let's just say I'm coldly indifferent."

"What you mean is," said Pavanaz, "that you'd like to try out my 'Vader, right? Live and let live? Forgive and forget?"

"I didn't say that," said Aces. "In fact I'd like to see you get your ass best! But I'm not the one who can do it to you, so in fact I'm not going to have *anything* to do with you. 'Cos you just don't smell right. Look after yourself, Parrotsquat." And he turned on his heel and left.

But the rest of them were putty in Pav's hands. He played for them; they *oohed* and *aahed*! He let them play, watched as they got blasted all over space. He was light-years ahead of them. Any fool could see that….

An hour later and it was time to close the place up. Pavanaz enlisted the aid of his worshippers to drag his 'Vader into a room Fat Bill was only too pleased to clear out for him, and before they left he said to them:

"Guys, I have an idea which I think you'll like. Kem, you'll like it best of all. A lot of you lost money tonight, creds you loaned to Aces and Kem here. Now I'm going to give you a chance to get those creds back."

"Big deal!" somebody groaned. "Pavanaz, we couldn't beat you in a thousand years! Win our money back? That's not the funniest thing you ever said."

"I didn't say 'win' it back," Pav sighed. "Who mentioned miracles? So why don't we talk about earning it back, eh?"

"Earn it back?" (This from Kem, who was learning caution.) "You mean we should work for you?"

Pavanaz shrugged. "You can call it that if you like. Me, I'd call it easy money. I mean, there are other arcades on this morass, right? Other 'champions'? So go on out there and bring 'em back alive! Bring 'em here, to me. Guys long on creds and short on talent—by my standards. And that covers everybody, you dig?"

"This is easy money?" someone piped up. "You rip 'em off, and we get beaten up? Easy money for who—Grint Pavanaz?"

Again Pavanaz sighed. "All you got right was my name," he said. "Look, why should they take it out on you? You think I want you to lie? Like you should tell them there's this nut called Pavanaz who's loaded and an easy mark for anyone with one good eye and a steady hand? Hell, no! Tell 'em the truth and nothing but—that I'm the best there is. That way, who could resist coming to see for himself? Could you? And for every hundred I take off one of these suckers, it's ten creds to the guy who reeled him in. Now tell me, is that easy money or isn't it?"

With which, no one could find anything to disagree.

III

It happened like Pavanaz figured: customers were shy; and business quiet—for forty-eight hours. Then word got out and the punters came in. At first from arcades on the spaceport perimeter, then from Guni, the supply town, eventually from halfway across Shankov's as Pavanaz's legend spread. By night five, his take was approaching four thousand credits and all debts paid, however grudgingly.

For this he'd had to lose the occasional game (the little ones, to give the punters heart) and the rest of the time he'd played as only Grint Pavanaz could, but not once extending himself too far. It was all good practice for the tournament.

Fat Bill was happy; Pav's pals were happy, including Kem; happiest of all was Pavanaz himself. A packet for Earth was due in a fortnight, and he'd made the down payment on a ticket for himself and a crate for his 'Vader. He needed another grand to buy his passage outright and give him floating creds to spare.

But the next day takings were down, and the day after that they fell away entirely. By the next morning Pavanaz was back to playing two credit games with the local talent, and already he suspected he wasn't going to make it. Only eleven days left and hopes rapidly fading, Pavanaz despaired. He'd been a shade too good, too greedy, too soon. That's what was wrong.

Noon of that same day, after Fat Bill went out for lunch, who should walk in but Aces with...somebody. Pavanaz knew he was somebody as soon as he saw him.

He was cleaning his 'Vader when the two came over. He heard Aces' sneakers on the tiled floor, but not the footsteps of the other. This one walked like a cat, looked like one, too. But an old cat, a mouser out of time. To Pav, anyone over thirty-five was ancient—history, almost—and this guy was ten plus beyond that. He looked like...a relic from the Khuum wars? In that last observation, Pavanaz couldn't be more accurate if he tried. Indeed Hal Gaddy *was* a relic from the Khuum wars.

"Aces," Pavanaz nodded, casually. "And...friend?"

"Pavanaz," said Aces, short on greetings, "this is Gaddy. He'd like to see you play. If he's impressed, maybe he'll let you try to take some money off him."

"Gee, I'm honored!" said Pavanaz.

"You should be," the newcomer growled, like gravel sliding down a chute. And Pavanaz looked at him more closely.

Hal Gaddy was five-seven in his high-heeled boots, weighed maybe a hundred and thirty-five pounds, and was tanned a permanent brown to match his trappings. While his jacket and trousers were of a fine, thin leather, his leather gloves looked almst painted on his hands. But inside those gloves Gaddy's hands themselves were trembling where they hung loosely, yet awkwardly, at his sides.

Gaddy's forearm under rolled-up sleeves were deeply scarred; likewise his face, which was equipped with eyes that were piercing blue and looked like cold moons rising behind the hollow crags of his weathered cheeks. His mouth was straight, but a small piece of his upper lip was missing on the left, letting an eye-tooth show through like naked bone. The many lines etched into his skin around his eyes and mouth could be from laughter or pain, Pav wasn't sure. He suspected, though, that Gaddy hadn't laughed in a long time.

"See," said Pavanaz after a moment, "it's a game of skill. Good eyes, hands, nerves, and an ability to anticipate bordering on the supernatural— that's all it takes. Over twenty-two or three and you're slowing down, twenty-five and you're plodding, more than that and you're in reverse. I see that back on Earth a sixteen-year-old black kid has run the first three-minutes-forty mile! Why don't you go in for athletics, Mr. Gaddy? I mean, your chances would be a lot better."

"Stow the mister," said Gaddy. "Call me Gunner."

Pavanaz knew what that meant and for a moment felt a genuine thrill. Gunner! If so, Gaddy was a fighter pilot from the Khuum wars. Or...he was a fake, a bum living someone else's legend for whatever crumbs got thrown his way. But the Khuum had pulled out a quarter-century ago, so it was just possible. *Just*, because surviving Gunners from that mess were so few you could count them on one hand with several fingers missing. So Pav had always understood it.

"The real thing, eh?" he said, finally nodding, but knowingly, cynically. "Maybe. Or...just another stowaway?"

"Stowaway?" Gaddy lifted an eyebrow.

"Sure." Pavanaz shrugged. "On Gizzich I knew a couple of 'Gunners.' One was a cook retired off cruisers, and the other was a colorblind son of a no-account prospector from Faggul V. But they'd read the manuals and you couldn't fault 'em—until they climbed into a bucket. Gunners? *Naw!* Just stowaways hitching a ride on a legend."

"Pavanaz, you're a—" Aces started forward, his jaw jutting.

"It's OK, son," said Gaddy, his chipped lip lifting a little. And to Pav: "I'd heard you had lots of mouth, Pavanaz, so that kind of garbage doesn't worry me. What? I should lose my cool just before a game?"

Pavanaz scowled. "Who said you were going to get one?"

Gaddy took out a five-credit note and waved it under Pav's nose. "This says so," he said. "Also the fact that you're dying to know. 'Cos if I'm the real thing, you're not going to meet another one in a long, long time."

"*Hah!*" Pavanaz snorted. "I should play for fives? Against grandfathers? For the thrill of gutting a tired old Gunner? *If* you're for real?"

"The word is," Aces grated, still sizzling, "you're down to playing for twos, hotshot."

"Well—" Pavanaz started, paused, and eventually continued, "—see, it's like this: the twos are for amusement. But five on a grudge is cheap and nasty. I mean, it *would* be a grudge game, right, Aces old buddy? You brought this guy in here to wipe the floor with me, to see me sweat for a miserable five, right? I'm not amused, and I'm not desperate either. But for fifty…?"

"Now that's greedy," said Gaddy, shaking his head. "That's a lot of credits. You're expensive, Pavanaz…but," he sighed and shrugged, "I'll go along with it—if you play first. See, it's rumored your 'Vader has a couple of embellishments, stuff the other machines don't have? And lord knows you've had plenty of practice, right? It seems only fair I should get to see what I'm up against."

"Like in the Khuum wars?" Pav made a gawping, idiot face. "They'd show you their hardware before a dogfight, right?" He laughed at Aces' raging expression, then sobered. "Fair enough. I go first and we play for fifty. And good ol' Aces here can hold the pot." He handed over his money and Gaddy matched it. And without more ado Pavanaz got aboard and opened her up.

He played hard but not too hard and clocked three million. But to do it he had to show almost everything the machine had. Gaddy knew what he was up against…from the machine if not from its owner. But Pav figured it like this: If Gaddy was the real thing and *if* he still had it, then maybe—just maybe—he could win. And of course he'd want to do it again. Except next time it would be for *real* money and Pavanaz would *really* play. And if Gaddy was a fraud…well maybe he'd come back for more anyway, especially if his score wasn't too far behind.

But it seemed that Gaddy was indeed faking it: he scored close to three million but not close enough, and Pavanaz pocketed the kitty. Glancing at

Gaddy out of the corner of his eye, he could see how choked he was. "If you can't stand losing," said Pavanaz, "then you really shouldn't gamble."

"Yeah?" Gaddy grunted. "Maybe. But for all your newfangled gewgaws, hell, I nearly had you!"

"Nearly doesn't cut it," said Pav.

At that Gaddy's lips tightened. "We go again!" he snapped, and Pavanaz got the feeling that even though this was what he'd intended, still it was a rerun of something or other.

"Oh yeah?" he said, playing it like always yet feeling it was playing him. "You can afford three hundred, can you, Gaddy? 'Cos that's what this one will cost you...three hundred *minimum*! Take it or leave it."

Gaddy took out a tight little roll and opened it up. Just three notes in there, but they were all Big Ones. Bigger than hundreds, certainly. Three grand, which he handed to Aces for safekeeping. And as the notes passed before Pav's eyes, Gaddy made sure he saw the zeroes. "Just to get the adrenalin flowing," he growled. "Can *you* afford it, Pavanaz?"

Pav's eyes bugged and he breathed a small sigh. It was all there: his ticket to Earth, his gateway to a pad on a beach on one of the resort worlds! Three thousand credits, the key to a million more! And this tired old man hadn't even seen him play yet. Not *really* play!

He counted his cash into Aces' hand, ventilated and hyperventilated his lungs, climbed yet again into the bucket. And as he switched her on, too late to stop and think again, suddenly he remembered something he'd said or thought: that Gaddy hadn't seen him play yet. But the fact was that *he* hadn't seen Gaddy play, either. The old guy had scored nearly three million, and never a drop of sweat. As for his shaky old hands: once they'd settled to the machine's controls, there hadn't been a single shake in 'em!

But too late because Pavanaz was into the game. And with three thousand credits and his entire future riding on it, he couldn't worry about anything now except survival—*his* survival, out among the cold, impersonal stars. And Pav played like never before, played it for real and for true and for life and for death, and for all of his past and all of his future, the future he'd killed for and would kill for again if necessary. Except it wasn't necessary, for he need only win this game.

And at seven million one thousand nine hundred and sixty, a shatterbeam found him and shivered his ship to shards. Pav, too, the way he slumped there in the bucket when it was over.

As they lifted him down, he groaned: "No need to play it off if you don't want to, old-timer. Let's face it, it would only be embarrassing. Aces, give me my money."

But Gaddy only told him, "Son, that was a good game and twenty-seven years ago we might have had a use for someone like you. Except you wouldn't have been interested because you're only interested in you. As for giving you the money: the eggs aren't hatched yet, Pavanaz." And then *he* played.

But where Pavanaz had only played for real, Gunner Gaddy played for *real.*

27102 Gunner Gaddy H, he'd been, "Khuum-Killer" to his friends, the young men who joined up and went out into space, and often as not didn't come back. Brief friends, anyway. But Gaddy had kept on coming back, so that he'd have been a legend if there'd been anyone keeping count of his missions. But when the going got rough even the Brass went out, and most of them didn't come back either. And the new Brass didn't know Gaddy at all: he was just another kid who killed Khuum and was destined to get killed himself, like all the rest.

Khuum-Killer Gaddy, he'd been then…and still was!

The patterns their ships made in space were familiar to Gaddy as the lines on his hands had…had used to be. That was before the aliens who saved his life gave him his gloves. Since then there'd been no lines on his hands at all, and when he took the gloves off….

But this wasn't the time or place to let that surface again. This was Khuum-killing time, and they knew he was there and were taking up defensive positions as he swept in towards them. No game, this, not for Gaddy, just a replay from life, a rerun of the only thing that had ever brought his mind fully alive and set the adrenalin in his blood to full flow. And yet not really a replay, either, for now his ship was that much more sophisticated and his weaponry so much more devastating. While the Khuum…why, they were just the same old bad old Khuum as always!

In a move the 'Vader didn't know it possessed, Gaddy spun his fighter end over end, howling through the Khuum ranks in a Catherine wheel of destruction, his fingers—no, his gloves—a blur of fluttering motion on the firing studs. Spinning like that, it appeared the Khuum were everywhere, and not a one of them who passed his crosshairs came out the other side! Then he was through them, killing his spin, sensing them reforming behind him, and tripping into hyperspace before they could fix their Warpers on him.

Back there in normal space they burned in his exhaust; but Gaddy was out of hyperspace just as quickly as in, looping back on himself, coming down on them where the dumb bastards opened up on his afterimage. They never knew what hit them, vaporizing all around him as he worked all his studs at once!

But so many Khuum fighters? What the hell?—they must be riding shotgun on something big, something huge! It was the 'Vader compensating, except Gaddy wasn't thinking 'Vader but death to the Khuum. The machine had never experienced so much computerized destruction so fast, and it was answering Gaddy the only way it could: by speeding up the game and bringing forward The End *that much faster. And to do so it was sticking up the Big Stuff on the screen, the invincible stuff, the stuff that carried the highest scores.*

But…something big, Gaddy thought. Something huge! *And yes, there it was!*

Cutting in his visiblizers, Gaddy saw its dull metallic gleam for a moment where the object furrowed space behind its No-see screens, false stars sliding along its vast hull stem to stern to make him think it was empty space. A battle-station!—a mother!—*launching carriers and tiny Khuum-manned suicide darts; and the carriers launching cruisers, mines, missiles; and the cruisers lining up their entropy torps; and the darts intent on death and glory, but mainly intent on nailing Gaddy. And all this hardware firming into reality as it came screaming out from under the battle-station's No-sees.*

The battle-station was impregnable to anything Gaddy had, but he knew how to get it. The station was about to launch its last carrier; Gaddy must get the carrier before it cleared the launch-tubes and threw up its screens. Twisting and writhing like light-speed snakes of green fire, the Takka-beams leaped the light-seconds to their target. Programmed to follow the beams, the Warp-torp zigzagged around and through everything the frantic Khuum tossed at it. The Takkas found the carrier, and a micro-second later so did the torp. The carrier, still sliding out of the battle-station's belly, warped out of existence like a small sun gone nova. And the battle-station had no option but to go nova with it!

"Got you, you bastard!" *Gaddy tried to scream, nothing coming out but a choking cough, his throat was* that *dry. But strange, because he did hear screams. Except…they weren't his.*

"No—no—*no!*" Pavanaz danced beside the 'Vader like some demented puppet-master's doll, clawed at the jiving bucket-seat and leaped up alongside, to wrench Gaddy's hands—no Gaddy's *gloves*—from the controls.

Gaddy was about to trip into hyperspace; with no one at the controls his ship tore into the battle-station's planet-wide fireball. Khuum disruptors followed it; stripped down its armor to an eggshell that withered in the nuclear furnace….

"No!" Pavanaz sobbed again, trying to drag Gaddy out of the bucket. "You've killed it! Jesus, you've *killed* it!" He didn't mean the battle-station.

"Killed it?" Gaddy got his straps loose, fell out of the seat, somehow managed to land on his feet. And again: "Killed it?" he said. He was still reeling a little, not yet back on solid ground. Snarling, Pavanaz grabbed his throat. And Aces hit him from the side, a blow that crushed his ear and deafened him on that side for two hours. But it also knocked him loose from Gunner Gaddy.

"His machine!" Aces said then, gasping, pointing at the 'Vader. While on the floor Pavanaz rocked and cried.

His 'Vader, yes, which he'd programmed to cave in if anyone took it over twenty million—because he'd known that no one could *ever* take it over twenty million. No one human, anyway. Unless it was him. But Gaddy had, and in so doing he'd killed it.

Twenty mill? The score, while it lasted, stood at *twenty-five million* and odds! The battle-station alone had been worth half of that! But who was counting? Pavanaz knew it would have been more if he hadn't interrupted the game. Not much more, because once past the Big Twenty and the self-destructs had started to cut in, systematically junking the whole machine. And right now the 'Vader's complex guts were going up in gray, stinking smoke and blue electrical fire, and the machine sputtered and sparked where she sat atop her own internal funeral pyre.

"Gaddy," said Aces, awed. "You...you've bust it!"

And because Pavanaz couldn't hear what Aces said, he couldn't contradict him—couldn't tell him that this had been his target, his impossible dream. Because he had known that if there ever came a time when *he* could clock twenty million, by then he'd be *worth* that much and it just wouldn't matter. But right now it mattered a lot. The 'Vader dying there was taking his whole world, his universe with it.

Pavanaz watched it go, then crawled into a corner and did a Kem job all over Fat Bill's not-so-immaculately-clean floor....

IV

When fat Bill sloshed back to the arcade after lunch he found his private door open and Grint Pavanaz sitting (or slumped) behind his desk, head thrown back and feet propped up on the imitation mahogany. He saw Pavanaz, then the door of the wall safe where it, too, stood open. For a fat man, Bill could move fast when he had to; his tiny electric stunner was dwarfed by his pudgy fist in less time than it takes to tell. "What...?" he wheezed then, his piggy gaze transferring from Pavanaz to the safe and back again. "What...?"

Finally Pavanaz looked at him. "Yes," he said listlessly. "What, what." And: "Don't panic, Bilbo, I didn't take anything. I was going to, but…it was depression, that's all. By the time I had the safe open, I could see how stupid it would be."

Fat Bill gawped, closed his mouth and snapped the fingers of his free hand. Being fat and wet, the sound was more a *plop* than a *snap*. "Aces and Gaddy!" he said. "I saw them down the street. When the rain started up, they took a cab. They were here. They took…you?"

Pavanaz's face was all twisted. "Gaddy did," he said, hurting to admit it. "That stinking rocket-jockey! But…I don't know how, I really don't know how! There *is* no one who can take me on—so how come I'm not nearly as good as him? It's driving me nuts!" Then he scowled. "More to the point, how come you didn't warn me about him—'partner'?" He looked accusingly at Bill.

"Tell you about him? Warn you? I ain't even *seen* the guy in years!" Fat Bill jutted his wobbly jaw. "He was dead for all I knew! And don't change the subject. What, you accusing *me* of stuff, and guilty as all get out? *And* my safe open?"

"It's safe," said Pavanaz humorlessly. And: "You'd better tell me about Gaddy. He has a secret, and I want it. Because if he has it, others might have it too. And I'm not going back to Earth to discover I'm last in line! I was the best, and with whatever it is he's got I'll be the best again."

Fat Bill crossed to his safe. "How much?" he said.

"I told you I didn't take anything!" Pav snapped. "What, and have you waiting for me at the embarkation with the local cops and a warrant? That's no way to get to Earth, and it's sure no way to win a million!"

"How much did *they* take off *you*, dummy!" Fat Bill snorted. And Pav didn't much like being talked to like that, but there was nothing he could do about it.

Fat Bill had just locked he safe and changed the combination when Pavanaz answered: "He took three thousand off me."

"*What!?*" The fat man's jaw fell open. "Three th—"

"Three grand—three biggies," Pavanaz cut him off. "And I fell for it like it was all new to me. And now I'm mad."

"But he beat you fair," said Fat Bill. "Fair's fair—and our partnership is dissolved. Out," he jerked his thumb. "And take your debris with you!"

Pavanaz didn't move. "How'd you like to make two hundred thou?" he said, slowly. "Two hundred grand, all for your fat little self??"

"I'm listening," Fat Bill answered, after a long moment. "But my attention span is shortening by the second."

"A million's what I'm set to win on Earth," said Pavanaz, "and twenty percent of that can be yours—partner?"

"A new partnership?" Fat Bill grimaced. "So soon? And I'm to get two hundred grand out of it? Who do you want killed, Pav?"

"Information," said Pavanaz, "that's all I want. And maybe—just maybe—a grubstake to Earth. Hell, you could squeeze it out of what I've already earned you!"

Fat Bill scowled. "Last time, I got forty percent."

"But that was peanuts," said Pav. "And this is creds!" He capitalized the last word. But as Fat Bill hesitated, he swung his legs down from the desk and stood up. "Why am I wasting my time?" he asked, of no one in particular. "People have seen me play. I can find a backer somewhere else."

"Hold it!" said Fat Bill as Pavanaz made to leave. "You'll sign a contract, making me your manager on twenty percent?"

"Damn right!" Pavanaz nodded.

"So, I may be crazy but…let's work it out," said the other. When they'd finished doing that, then he began to talk in earnest.…

"Gaddy was a ground staff mechanic in the Corps," (said Fat Bill), "just a kid who patched up fighters when they got shot up. His girl and her folks lived here on Shankov's—on the other side—in a little mountain township that got more than its fair share of sunlight by virtue of its elevation. It got a lot of exposure to the Khuum, too. The night Gaddy and his girl got married, in one of the cities *under* the cloud layer, the Khuum took out her village. For no good reason; it wasn't tactical or in support or anything; just the Khuum being the Khuum. Her folks died. But…it was like they were Gaddy's folks, too.

"After that Gaddy was changed. He became a Gunner—for the duration. He survived because there was a girl to come back to, and because there were Khuum to keep going after. He led a love-hate life, you know? Out scouting one time, he came across a gaggle of Khuum bandits attacking an alien ship. But I'm talking *alien!* He'd never seen anything like it before, it was that weird. And no one ever saw anything like it since. It must have been sort of just passing through this sector.

"That alien ship was in a bad way, crippled, its shields going down like dominoes. Gaddy didn't know if it was friendly or what, but he knew how he felt about the Khuum. He went in, took the bandits by surprise and played all hell with them—which gave the alien ship time to get itself operational again and back in the action. Gaddy'd cut the Khuum pack down to just three when finally one of them got him and burned his fighter. He was cut up and burned, too, but he managed to eject. Spinning in space, he saw the alien ship open up with one godawful weapon that erased those three Khuum fighters like chalk off a blackboard! Then he passed out....

"When he came round he was inside the alien ship and they were working on him, putting him right. He saw the mess he was in—mainly his hands—and passed out again. But they fixed him up with those gloves of his, put him in a life-support pod and dropped him just inside the Corps radius. Our boys picked up the alien ship on their scanners, and when they went for a look-see found Gaddy.

He asked for out and the Corps let him go. Hell, he'd done his bit, and maybe he'd finally figured out just how lucky he'd been. The Khuum were retreating by then, and the sheer *science* that came out of Gaddy's alien life-support pod put the finishing touches to it. A year later the war was over, and the Khuum had backed off wherever they'd come from.

"Gaddy came back to Shankov's; eventually he and his woman had their baby son—Aces. But the girl hadn't been the same since her folks got theirs. She died young and Gaddy was left on his own with the kid. He raised him, turned him loose when he was seventeen, then dropped out of sight. Sort of retired himself—from everything. That was two or three years ago.

"And that's about as much as I know. I got it in bits and pieces here and there—with difficulty. See, people respect Gaddy; they let him alone. The way I see what happened here today, Aces was really kissed off and cajoled his father into taking you down a peg."

Pavanaz nodded sourly. "Not hard to figure," he said. And then he frowned. "So his hands were burned up, right? And the aliens gave him those gloves?"

"You got it. And he's never been seen without 'em."

"Aliens," said Pav, still frowning, "with weapons and an advanced technology we can't even guess at. They were passing through and got in trouble; Gaddy pulled their nuts out of the fire; he got burned doing it, so they squared it by...*that's it*! They made sure he came out of it better than when he went in!"

"Sure," Fat Bill shrugged, having figured it out for himself. "Naturally. He has hi-tec fingers."

"He cheated me!" Pavanaz was furious.

"Hell, no," said Fat Bill. "You ever done target shooting? You can't disqualify a man just because he's better equipped!"

"The way *I* see it he cheated," Pav insisted. "Where does he live?"

"Now wait!" Fat Bill was alarmed. "Twenty percent of murder I can do without!"

"I don't want his life," Pavanaz snorted (though he really wouldn't mind, if he could do it smart), "I want his skill, his edge. Shit, the war's over! He doesn't need it—but I do!"

"Let it be, kid," said Fat Bill. "He's outgunned you once. Gaddy's no fool."

"Does he live with Aces?"

Fat Bill shook his head. "Like I told you, they parted company when Aces got himself a job here in the spaceport. The kid lives right here, but Gaddy lives way out. On his own. He was a one-woman guy."

"Where?" Pavanaz demanded.

And sighing, Fat Bill told him. Hell, it was Pav's neck.

After the Khuum wars, the Corps had taken care of its men. It could afford to; not too many had come through it. Also, Gaddy must have picked up a disability pension. (The thought of *that* almost made Pavanaz scream!)

Property hadn't been so expensive then; not on a swamp like Shankov's, which made Gizzich IV seem positively dry! Gaddy had bought himself a house surrounded by waterways. Not for security (after the Khuum, what was there to feel insecure about?), just for peace of mind. He hadn't wanted hassle, and the only people he'd needed were his people. After his wife died he'd lived with Aces, and now he was on his own.

Following Fat Bill's directions, Pav had covered the eight hundred miles to Gaddy's locality by jet-boat and steam-paddle, taking two days and a night to get there. Arriving in the local town on the evening of the second day, he'd hired a fan-driven swamp-skimmer (he was an off-worlder, here for the fishing). As darkness came down, he'd located Gaddy's address. Then, putting out a dummy fishing line, he'd slept on board the skimmer for a few hours, coming awake at 2:00 a.m. in the morning. It was eerily quiet and all Gaddy's lights were out.

There was a wooden bridge over the canal to the house, but Pav didn't want to take the chance someone would see him crossing. So he wrapped the skimmer's breakdown oars and paddled silently across, then moored his boat in the mangroves on the rim of Gaddy's property. Pav was equipped for a break-in but it wasn't necessary—the place was wide open.

In the entrance porch he took off his shoes, put on clean cloth shuf-flers, then crept into the main building. There were only a few internal doors, none locked; inside was as eerie and as quiet as out; security was literally nonexistent. The place was mainly a solarium (synthetic sunlight, which switched itself off nights), and a greenhouse where Gaddy gardened. Exotic plants crept all over the place, not just adding to but mainly being the décor. It was a big house and, Pav supposed, lonely.

He carried a life-seek whose winking red indicator led him to Gaddy's bedroom, a huge, high-ceilinged, opaque glass-walled room with a big double bed in the middle; and Gaddy was in it, just his hair showing, asleep, dreaming…and moaning. Whatever he was dreaming, it wasn't good stuff.

Gaddy's clothes were all over a curving bamboo couch, and his gloves were lying on top of the other things. It was easy as that. Pavanaz took the gloves and tucked them in his shirt.

On his way out he looked into a side room. It had been a games room of sorts, though long out of use. There was a pool table in there, its green baize dark with dust, an antique 20th Century one-armed bandit, a dartsboard rotting in its frame on the wall, and…a 'Vader. But the machine was all of thirty years out of date. This was what Aces must have practiced on when he was kid, and it explained two things: why he was so good, and why he wasn't good enough.

Pavanaz didn't bother looking at anything else but picked up his shoes, paddled a quarter-mile off in his skimmer, then fanned it back to Bogside Bassum and the hotel room he'd taken there. After he locked the door, then he took out the gloves. And just looking at them he knew that he was right, that this was where Gaddy got his magic, his unbeatable 'Vader wizardry. The gloves were…they were just…alien!

Pavanaz sat on his bed and looked at them, examined what he could of them, tougher than good quality leather, and grained like leather, too— he'd never seen anything like them. They were long enough to come halfway up a man's forearms, and they matched the rest of Gaddy's kit, the leather he'd worn as a Gunner. The aliens had made them that way with their strange science.

That was the gloves on the outside, but inside they were stranger still. Pavanaz shook one and blew into it, and *looked* into it—and saw nothing. It was like space in there, just an empty hole. Even shining a torch inside, there was only darkness. Light didn't penetrate, nor would they turn inside out. Tug and twist all you like, they'd spring back to their original shape. Pavanaz grinned, because now he was *sure* he had Gaddy's number. All that remained was to put the gloves on.

Which he did….

What it was he expected to feel would be difficult to say. A quickening of his senses? A tingling in his fingertips presaging reactions fast as lightning? A sudden awareness that the only thing in the universe faster and more adroit and slippery than his hands would be a couple of snakes screwing in hyperspace? Something of all these things, he supposed, but it wasn't what he got.

He got pain. A burning pain, like his hands were roasting, but slowly.

And as the pain gradually increased, so Pav remembered the lines he'd seen on Gaddy's face, which he hadn't supposed to be laughter lines. He went to take the gloves off—and couldn't!

They wouldn't peel; there was no rim he could get hold of; his hands were hot as hell in there, and the gloves were sticking like glue! He ran cold water in a bowl; plunged his hands into it. No good. The gloves weren't hot, they only *felt* hot. Hold them to his face and they were cool. It was his *hands* that were hot, and maybe not even that. It was the pain *itself* that was hot!

Pav almost panicked then, but he remembered who he was and what he'd done, and the stakes he was playing for. This hurting was just part of the process, that was all. That must be right: the pain was the gloves transferring their power to him. It was his initiation. They wouldn't come off till they were ready to, until he and they went together…hand in glove?

But they *must* come off, eventually, because Gaddy had taken them off. So the frurking things weren't permanent—were they? *Were* they? But the pain! The godawful, screaming, acid-etched *pain*! His hands felt like they were melting!

Pav called the desk to send out for painkillers, and when they came he took three times the recommended dose. The pain eased off…a little, and when he'd stopped shaking and panting and could think straight, he tried once more to take the gloves off. Still they wouldn't come. He tried tugging at the fingertips, rolling down the cuffs, sliding them off between his thighs—everything. And nothing. They wouldn't budge.

So…he would have to see what the morning brought. And morning was just three hours away now. Taking a second handful of pills, finally Pavanaz fell into a troubled sleep….

V

Pavanaz dreamed he held his hands up before his face, and the tips of his fingers and thumbs blew off like the lids of tiny volcanoes and shot boiling blood all over him!

He started awake and the pain was back, and he lay in the sweat of his agonized tossing and turning. The pain had probably been there all the time, but like a toothache it wasn't so bad when you were asleep. Pav swallowed the rest of his pills, got dressed, checked himself out in the mirror. His young face was lined like never before. *God!* he thought, *I'm aging a day in an hour!* Every hour of the pain in his hands.

He examined the gloves. The way his hands felt in there, they should have melted down by now, developed into shapeless blobs. They should be pulsating, and issuing slop from blisters that came bursting right through the alien material. But...they weren't. Nothing had changed. Pav's hands in Gaddy's gloves were the same size and shape as always. Just as dexterous, and just as—

Pavanaz felt his flesh creep, the short hairs at the back of his neck stirring—in awe and wonder as yet. In something of triumph, too, however depleted by the pain. And his eyebrows came together and down in a scowling squint as he gazed at the gloves. Because his hands weren't "just as" but *more* dexterous! Somehow, he just knew that he could use his fingers, thumbs and hands faster, more cleverly, than ever before. They were more supple, more alive, more...*painful!*

He examined the gloves again. Last night there'd been no cuffs. The material had gripped the skin of his forearm like it was melded to them, without constricting or cutting. Like a wide elastic band, but without restricting his circulation. This morning, there were cuffs, gaps between the material and the flesh of his forearms, forming narrow bells into which his hands disappeared. Pav at once tried to take the gloves off by rolling down the cuffs, but they wouldn't come. Two inches down towards the wrists, the material was joined to his flesh.

He got his thumbnail in and tried slicing the material from his skin, which only increased the pain. Frustrated beyond endurance, he wrenched at the right-hand glove, bunching its cuff in the curl of the smallest and second fingers of his left hand and trying to tear it free—which really *was* painful! Weakened by the agony welling out of his hands and flooding his mind and body, he staggered back against the bed and fell onto it. And a trickle of red escaped from beneath the cuff of Gaddy's glove! A few drops from a patch of torn skin, but to Pavanaz it was like his life leaking away. He knew he'd done the damage himself, but still it was as if those frurking gloves were eating him!

At which, something snapped in Pav; not his mind but his resolve. Fear sprang up stronger than ambition, and agony overcame avarice. Only one man could get these terrible gloves off his hands without damaging them, and that was their owner, Gunner Gaddy....

Pav left the hotel, found an all-night store and bought more pills and a gutting knife with an edge keen as a razor, and went right back to Gaddy's place. In the misty dawn light he tied up his skimmer at the wharf, climbed to the bridge and crossed it. If Gaddy was up he might see him…so what? He was going to wake the bastard anyway. Wake him up, learn the secret of the gloves, slit his throat and sink him deep. The fish would do the rest. But thank God (in whom Pav never had believed) *thank God* he hadn't killed him last night!

He entered the house as before, put on shufflers, went straight to Gaddy's bedroom. And there was the man himself: yawning, sitting up in his bed with his hands under the covers, peering all about in the dull dawn glow coming through the glass ceiling. Gaddy saw Pavanaz—and gave a huge start when he recognized the gloves he wore. He seemed to see only the gloves, not the ugly knife Pav carried in the one on the right. Then the startled look left Gaddy's cat face and he glanced knowingly at his clothes piled on the bamboo couch. Following which he returned his gaze to Pavanaz.

"Something I can do for you, son?" he inquired, softly.

"You can tell me about these," Pavanaz answered, holding up his gloved hands. Then he switched on the lamps and flooded the room with sunlight, and moved closer to the bed. "And you can do it quick before I pin you to that bedhead!" Now Gaddy saw the knife, or at least acknowledged it.

"Murder?" he said.

"Only if I have to," Pavanaz lied through his teeth—and moaned through them too, as the pain started up again. Moaned like Gaddy had been moaning during his bad dream last night.

"You don't look too well, son," said Gaddy, in a voice that really couldn't care less.

But the pain had subsided a little and Pav spun the knife in the air in a blur of sharp steel, and caught it expertly by the tip of its scalloped blade. "What the gloves did for you," he said, "they're doing it now for me. I could take off one of your ears from here, or punch a slot through one of your eyes, before you even registered that I'd moved."

"Are the gloves hurting you?" said Gaddy.

"Don't you just know it!" Pav grated. "So you can start by telling me why, and how long before it stops."

"I take it you know how I got them?" Gaddy sat up.

Pavanaz nodded, stepped closer to the bed. "I know how," he said. "Quit stalling. I asked you why they hurt, and when do they stop?"

Suddenly Gaddy's expression was sour. "Aliens fixed me up with those gloves," he said. "An alien medic gave them to me, 'cos they were the best he could do in the short time he had. I've thought about it a lot. Maybe those guys don't feel pain like we do. I mean, why would they save my life, and leave me in agony the rest of my days? So maybe pain isn't the same to them. Or…perhaps their flesh is different, compatible with that sort of surgery."

"Surgery?" Pav shook his head a little, to chase the pain away. "You're losing me. Are you telling me these things *never* stop hurting? Is that what you're saying?"

"Oh, you can stop them hurting," Gaddy answered. "Sure you can! That's as easy as taking them off."

"That was my next question," Pav sighed his relief, "just how do I take them off?"

But Gaddy's face was suddenly white. Distantly, he said: "I remember when I had the same problem. But in your case…I'm not sure. I can only imagine they'd work the same for you as for me."

"And how's that?" Pavanaz demanded.

And Gaddy shrugged, grimaced, and lifted his arms out from under the covers, to show Pavanaz how.

Pav's brain searched for words but nothing came out of his wide-open mouth. He half-sat, half-collapsed onto the bed and looked at Gaddy's hands, or what he had where hands should be: corkscrews of white flesh with blue veins showing through, ending in blunt points where sculpted bone had closed off the marrow cores! *Gaddy's "hands" had screw threads!*

"J…J…*Jesus!*" Pavanaz gasped then, letting his knife fall from nerveless (and what else?) fingers.

"You unscrew them," said Gaddy. "Left-hand thread…."

"But—" Pavanaz gulped, gazing wide-eyed, morbidly at the gloves on his hands. "But…your hands were ruined, and mine are good, whole."

"You're sure about that?" said Gaddy, logically. "Maybe the gloves assumed they weren't. Maybe they needed fixing…."

"Oh, Jesus!—*Jesus!*" Pav gabbled. He gave the right-hand glove a tentative twist—and it turned! And eyes bugging, Pavanaz unscrewed it all the way and let it fall. Even before it hit the covers the glove was just a glove again, limp and flexible and empty. But Pavanaz's hand wasn't a hand. It was one of the things Gaddy had—the thing he was now sliding into his glove, which filled out and swiftly screwed itself into place.

If Pavanaz saw any of that it didn't register; nothing registered but the fact that his good right hand was a screw. And…his left?

Gaddy said: "Here, let me help you." And he unscrewed the other glove from Pavanaz's wrist.

Pavanaz looked at both of his screws through eyes that threatened to come right out of his head. He gurgled and gasped and said nothing, and in the silence Gaddy got out of bed and dressed himself. And then Pavanaz's senses returned to him, at least partially. He lunged for the knife and couldn't pick it up, couldn't grab at anything to stop himself flying headlong across the bed. And now, in the absence of pain, his brain was working perfectly again.

"One of them," he gasped finally, his eyes full of pleading. "You'll give me—I'll buy—just one of them…?"

But Gaddy shook his head. "The gloves are mine, kid. I earned them. And anyway, you couldn't stand it. The only time I don't hurt is when I take them off and climb into bed. And then I dream I'm hurting."

"But *you* can stand it. So why not me?"

"We're not built the same," said Gaddy. "And anyway, I've got used to it—almost."

"But—"

"I'm taking you in," Gaddy cut him off. "The police will have to figure out what's to be done with you. And afterwards…they can do wonderful things these days, Pavanaz. You'll have hands again. Clumsy, maybe, but hands. Of sorts…."

Halfway across the bridge it all came crashing down on Pav. His dream blew itself away in his head. You can't be a champion and win a million with plastic fingers that don't feel anything. He turned abruptly and faced Gaddy, and without emotion said: "Frurk you." And he lifted his arms high and brought his screws crashing down on the hardwood handrail.

Hot blood splashed scarlet where altered flesh split open; and before Gaddy could do anything to stop it, if he wanted to, Pav flopped over the rail and down into the water. He surfaced once and screamed high and thin, went down in crimson foam and didn't surface again. And Gaddy turned away….

Drop a bent pin in the water on Shankov's and you'll pull out a fish. Put something edible on the hook…and the water boils.

★ ⁑★ ★

Big "C"

Also written in 1988, "Big 'C'" appeared two years later in a
TOR Books anthology of stories written "after" the Old Gent of
Providence, titled *Lovecraft's Legacy*. In this tale our protagonist
not only boldly goes but he also makes it back in one piece...
albeit in one big and very terrifying piece.

Now say, do you remember how H. P. Lovecraft's *Color Out
of Space* changed everything it touched? Of course you do, and
I'll say no more....

TWO THOUSAND THIRTEEN and the exploration of space—by men,
not robot spaceships—was well underway. Men had built Moonbase, landed
on Mars, were now looking towards Titan, though that was still some way
ahead. But then, from a Darkside observatory, Luna II was discovered half a
million miles out: a black rock two hundred yards long and eighty through,
tumbling dizzily end over end around the Earth, too small to occlude stars for
more than a blip, too dark to have been (previously) anything but the tiniest
sunspot on the surface of Sol. But interesting anyway "because it was there,"
and also and especially because on those rare occasions when it lined itself up
with the full moon, that would be when Earth's lunatics gave full vent.
Lunatics of all persuasions, whether they were in madhouses or White
Houses, asylums or the army, refuges or radiation shelters, surgeries or silos.

Men had known for a long time that the moon controlled the tides—
and possibly the fluids in men's brains?—and it was interesting now to
note that Luna II appeared to compound the offence. It seemed reasonable
to suppose that we had finally discovered the reason for Man's homicidal
tendencies, his immemorial hostility to Man.

Two thousand fifteen and a joint mission—American, Russian,
British—went to take a look; they circled Luna II at a "safe" distance for

twelve hours, took pictures, made recordings, measured radiation levels. When they came back, within a month of their return, one of the two Americans (the most outspoken one) went mad, one of the two Russians (the introverted one) set fire to himself, and the two British members remained phlegmatic, naturally.

One year later in August 2016, an Anglo-French expedition set out to double-check the findings of the first mission: i.e., to see if there were indeed "peculiar radiations" being emitted by Luna II. It was a four-man team; they were all volunteers and wore lead baffles of various thicknesses in their helmets. And afterwards, the ones with the least lead were discovered to be more prone to mental fluctuations. But…the "radiations," or whatever, couldn't be measured by any of Man's instruments. What was required was a special sort of volunteer, someone actually to land on Luna II and dig around a little, and do some work right there on top of—whatever it was.

Where to land wasn't a problem: with a rotation period of one minute, Luna II's equatorial tips were moving about as fast as a man could run, but at its "poles" the planetoid was turning in a very gentle circle. And that's where Benjamin "Smiler" Williams set down. He had wanted to do the job and was the obvious choice. He was a Brit riding an American rocket paid for by the French and Russians. (Everybody had wanted to be in on it.) And of course he was a hero. And he was dying of cancer.

Smiler drilled holes in Luna II, set off small explosions in the holes, collected dust and debris and exhaust gasses from the explosions, slid his baffles aside and exposed his brain to whatever, walked around quite a bit and sat down and thought things, and sometimes just sat. And all in all he was there long enough to see the Earth turn one complete circle on her axis—following which he went home. First to Moonbase, finally to Earth. Went home to die—after they'd checked him out, of course.

But that was six years ago and he still hadn't died (though God knows we'd tried the best we could to kill him) and now I was on my way to pay him a visit. On my way through him, traveling into him, journeying to his very heart. The heart and mind—the living, thinking organism, the control centre, as it were—deep within the body of what the world now called Big "C." July 2024, and Smiler Williams had asked for a visitor. I was it, and as I drove in I went over everything that had led up to this moment. It was as good a way as any to keep from looking at the "landscape" outside the car. This was Florida and it was the middle of the month, but I wasn't using the air-conditioning and in fact I'd even turned up the heater a little— because it was cool out there. As cool as driving down a country lane in

Devon, with the trees arching their green canopy overhead. Except it wasn't Devon and they weren't green. And in fact they weren't even trees....

Those were thoughts I should try to avoid, however, just as I avoided looking at anything except the road unwinding under the wheels of my car; and so I went back again to 2016, when Ben Williams came back from space.

The specialists in London checked Smiler out—his brain, mostly, for they weren't really interested in his cancer. That was right through him, (with the possible exception of his gray matter), and there was no hope. Try to cut or laser *that* out of him and there'd be precious little of the man himself left! But after ten days of tests they'd found nothing, and Smiler was getting restless.

"Peter," he said to me, "I'm short on time and these monkeys are wasting what little I've got left! Can't you get me out of here? There are places I want to go, friends I want to say goodbye to." But if I make that sound sad or melodramatic, forget it. Smiler wasn't like that. He'd really *earned* his nickname, that good old boy, because right through everything he'd kept on smiling like it was painted on his face. Maybe it was his way to keep from crying. Twenty-seven years old just a month ago, and he'd never make twenty-eight. So we'd all reckoned.

Myself, I'd never made it through training, but Smiler had and we'd kept in touch. But just because I couldn't go into space didn't mean I couldn't help others to do it, I'd worked at NASA, and on the European Space Program (ESP), even for a while for the Soviets at Baikonur, when *détente* had been peaking a periodic up-surge back in 2009 and 2010. So I knew my stuff. And I knew the men who were doing it, landing on Mars and what have you, and the heroes like Smiler Williams. So while Smiler was moderately cool toward the others on the space medicine team— the Frogs, Sovs and even the other Americans—to me he was the same as always. We'd been friends and Smiler had never let down a friend in his life.

And when he'd asked for my help in getting him out of that place, I'd had to go along with him. "Sure, why not?" I'd told him. "Maybe I can speed it up. Have you seen the new Space Center at the Lake? There are a lot of people you used to know there. NASA people. They'd love to see you again, Smiler."

What I didn't say was that the Space Center at Lake Okeechobee also housed the finest space medicine team in the world, and that they were longing to get their hands on him. But he was dying and a Brit, and so the British had first claim, so to speak. No one was going to argue the pros and cons about a man on his last legs. And if that makes me sound bad—like maybe I'd gone over to London to snatch him for the home team—I'd better add that there was something else I hadn't mentioned to him: the Center Research Foundation at Lakeport, right next door. I wanted to wheel him in there so they could take a look at him. Oh, he was a no-hoper, like I've said, but….

And maybe he hadn't quite given up hope himself, either, because when they were finally through with him a few days later he'd agreed to come back here with me. "What the hell," he'd shrugged. "They have their rocks, dust, gasses, don't they? Also, they have lots of time. Me, I have to use mine pretty sparingly." It was starting to get to him.

In the States Smiler got a hero's welcome, met everybody who was anybody from the President down. But that was time-consuming stuff, so after a few days we moved on down to Florida. First things first: I told him about the Foundation at Lakeport. "So what's new?" he laughed. "Why'd you think I came with you, Yank?"

They checked him over, smiled and joked with him (which was the only way to play it with Smiler) but right up front shook their heads and told him no, there was nothing they could do. And time was narrowing down.

But it was running out for me, too; and that's where I had to switch my memories off and come back to the present a while, for I'd reached the first checkpoint. I was driving up from Immokalee, Big "C" Control ("control," that's a laugh!) Point Seven, to see Smiler at Lakeport. The barrier was at the La Belle-Clewiston crossroads, and Smiler came up on the air just as I saw it up ahead and started to slow her down a little.

"You're two minutes early, Peter," his voice crackled out of the radio at me. "Try to get it right from here on in, OK? Big "C" said ten-thirty A.M. at the La Belle-Clewiston crossroads, and he didn't mean ten-twenty-eight. You don't gain anything by being early: he'll only hold you up down there two minutes longer to put you back on schedule. Do you read me, old friend?"

"I read you, buddy," I answered, slowing to a halt at the barrier's massive red-and-white-striped pole where it cut the road in half. "Sorry I'm early; I guess it's nerves; must have put my foot down a little. Anyway, what's a couple minutes between friends, eh?"

"Between you and me? Nothing!" Smiler's voice came back—and with a chuckle in it! I thought: *God, that's courage for you!* "But Big 'C' likes accuracy, dead reckoning," he continued. "And come to think of it, so do I! Hell, you wouldn't try to find me a reentry window a couple of minutes ahead of time, would you? No you wouldn't." And then, more quietly: "And remember, Peter, a man can get burned just as easily in here…." But this time there was no chuckle.

"What now?" I sat still, staring straight ahead, aware that the—tunnel?—was closing overhead, that the light was going as Big "C" enclosed me.

"Out," he answered at once, "so he can take a good look at the car. You know he's not much for trusting people, Peter."

I froze, and remained sitting there as rigid as…as the great steel barrier pole right there in front of me. Get out? Big "C" wanted me to get out? But the car was my womb and I wasn't programmed to be born yet, not until I got to Smiler. And—

"Out!" Smiler's voice crackled on the air. "He says you're not moving and it bothers him. So get out now—or would you rather sit tight and have him come in there with you? How do you think you'd like that, Peter: having Big "C" groping around in there with you?"

I unfroze, opened the car door. But where was I supposed to—?

"The checkpoint shack," Smiler told me, as if reading my mind. "There's nothing of him in there."

Thank God for that!

I left the car door open—to appease Big "C"? To facilitate his search? To make up for earlier inadequacies? Don't ask me—and hurried in the deepening gloom to the wooden, chalet-style building at the side of the road. It had been built there maybe four years ago when Big "C" wasn't so big, but no one had used it in a long time and the door was stuck; I could get the bottom of the door to give a little by leaning my thigh against it, but the top was jammed tight. And somehow I didn't like to make too much noise.

Standing there with the doorknob clenched tight in my hand, I steeled myself, glanced up at the ceiling being formed of Big "C"'s substance—the moth-eaten holes being bridged by doughy flaps, then sealed as the mass thickened up, shutting out the light—and I thought of myself as becoming a tiny shriveled kernel in his gigantic, leprous walnut. Christ…what a mercy I never suffered from claustrophobia! But then I also thought: *to hell with the noise*, and put my shoulder to the door to burst it right in.

I left the door vibrating in its frame behind me and went unsteadily, breathlessly, to the big windows. There was a desk there, chairs, a few well-thumbed paperbacks, a Daily Occurrence Book, telephone and scribble pad: everything a quarter-inch thick in dust. But I blew the dust off one of the chairs and sat (which wasn't a bad idea, my legs were shaking so bad), for now that I'd started in on this thing I knew there'd be no stopping it, and what was going on out there was all part of it. Smiler's knowledge of cars hadn't been much to mention; I had to hope that Big "C" was equally ignorant.

And so I sat there trembling by the big windows, looking out at the road and the barrier and the car, and I suppose the idea was that I was going to watch Big "C"'s inspection. I did actually watch the start of it—the tendrils of frothy slop elongating themselves downwards from above and inwards from both sides, closing on the car, entering it; a pseudopod of slime hardening into rubber, pulling loose the weather strip from the boot cover and flattening itself to squeeze inside; another member like a long, flat tapeworm sliding through the gap between the hood and the radiator grille...but that was as much as I could take and I turned my face away.

It's not so much how Big "C" looks but what he is that does it. It's knowing, and yet not really knowing, what he is....

So I sweated it there and waited for it to get done, and hoped and prayed that Big "C" *would* get done and not find anything. And while I waited my mind went back again to that time six years earlier.

The months went by and Smiler weakened a little. He got to spending a lot of his time at Lakeport, which was fine by the space medics at the Lake because they could go and see him any time they wanted and carry on examining and testing him. And at the time I thought they'd actually found something they could do for him, because after a while he really did seem to be improving again. Meanwhile I had my own life to live; I hadn't seen as much of him as I might like; I'd been busy on the Saturn's Moons Project.

When I did get to see him almost a year had gone by and he should have been dead. But he wasn't anything like dead and the boys from Med. were excited about something—had been for months—and Smiler had asked to see me. I was briefed and they told me not to excite him a lot, just treat him like...normal? Now how the hell else would I treat him? I wondered.

It was summer and we met at Clewiston on the Lake, a beach where the sun sparkled on the water and leisure craft came and went, many of them towing their golden, waving water-skiers. Smiler arrived from Lakeport in an ambulance and the boys in white walked him slowly down to the table under a sun umbrella where I was waiting for him. And I saw how big he was under his robe.

I ordered a Coke for myself, and—"Four vodkas and a small tomato juice," Smiler told me! "An Anemic Mary—in one big glass."

"Do you have a problem, buddy?" the words escaped me before I could check them.

"Are you kidding?" he said, frowning. But then he saw me ogling his huge drink and grinned. "Eh? The booze? Jesus, no! It's like rocket fuel to me—keeps me aloft and propels me around and around—but doesn't make me dizzy!" And then he was serious again. "A pity, really, 'cos there are times when I'd like to get blasted out of my mind."

"What?" I stared hard at him, wondered what was going on in his head. "Smiler, I—"

"Peter," he cut me short, "I'm not going to die—not just yet, anyway." For a moment I couldn't take it in, couldn't believe it. I was *that* delighted. I knew my bottom jaw must have fallen open, so closed it again. "They've come up with something?" I finally blurted it out. "Smiler, you've done it—you've beaten the Big 'C'!"

But he wasn't laughing or even smiling, just sitting there looking at me.

He had been all dark and lean and muscular, Smiler, but was now pale and puffy. Puffy cheeks, puffy bags under his eyes, pale and puffy double chins. And bald (all that shining, jet-black hair gone) and minus his eyebrows: the effect of one treatment or another. His natural teeth were gone, too: calcium deficiency brought on by low grav during too many missions in the space stations, probably aggravated by his complaint. In fact his eyes were really the only things I'd know him by: film-star blue eyes, which had somehow retained their old twinkle.

Though right now, as I've said, he wasn't laughing or even smiling but just sitting there staring at me.

"Big 'C,' " he finally answered me. "Beaten the Big 'C'...."

And eventually the smile fell from my face, too. "But...isn't that what you meant?"

"Listen," he said, suddenly shifting to a higher gear, "I'm short of time. They're checking me over every couple of hours now, because they're expecting it to break loose...well, soon. And so they'll not be too long coming for me, wanting to take me back into that good old 'controlled environment,' you know? So now I want to tell you about it—the way I see it, anyway."

"Tell me about...?"

"About Luna II. Peter, it was Luna II. It wasn't anything the people at Lakeport have done or the space medicine buffs from the Lake, it was just Luna II. There's something in Luna II that changes things. That's its nature: to change things. Sometimes the changes may be radical: it takes a sane man and makes him mad, or turns a peaceful race into a mindless gang of mass murderers, or changes a small planet into a chunk of shiny black slag that we've named Luna II. And sometimes it's sleeping or inert, and then there's no effect whatever."

I tried to take all of this in but it was coming too thick and fast. "Eh? Something in Luna II? But don't we already know about that? That it's a source of peculiar emanations or whatever?"

"Something like that." He shrugged helplessly, impatiently. "Maybe. I don't know. But when I was up there I felt it, and now it's starting to look like it felt me."

"It felt you?" Now he really *wasn't* making sense, had started to ramble.

"I don't know"—he shrugged again—"but it could be the answer to Everything—it could *be* Everything! Maybe there are lots of Luna IIs scattered through the universe, and they all have the power to change things. Like they're catalysts. They cause mutations—in space, in time. A couple of billion years ago the Earth felt it up there, felt its nearness, its effect. And it took this formless blob of mud hurtling through space and changed it, gave it life, brought microorganisms awake in the soup of its oceans. It's been changing things ever since—and we've called *that* evolution! Do you see what I mean? It was The Beginning—and it might yet be The End."

"Smiler, I—"

He caught my arm, gave me what I suspect was the most serious look he'd ever given anyone in his entire life, and said: "Don't look at me like that, Peter." And there was just a hint of accusation.

"Was I?"

"Yes, you were!" And then he relaxed and laughed, and just as suddenly became excited. "Man, when something like this happens, you're bound to ask questions. So I've asked myself questions, and the things I've told you are the answers. Some of them, anyway. Hell, they may not even be right, but they're my answers!"

"These are your thoughts, then? Not the boffins'?" This was one of his Brit words I used, from the old days. It meant "experts."

"Mine," he said, seeming proud of it, "but grown at least in part from what the boffins have told me."

"So what *has* happened?" I asked him, feeling a little exasperated now. "What's going down, Smiler?"

"Not so much going down," he shook his head, "as coming out."

"Coming out?" I waited, not sure whether to smile or frown, not knowing what to do or say.

"Of me."

And still I waited. It was like a guessing game where I was supposed to come up with some sort of conclusion based on what he'd told me. But I didn't have any conclusions.

Finally he shrugged yet again, snorted, shook his head, and said: "But you do know about cancer, right? About the Big 'C'? Well, when I went up to Luna II, it changed my cancer. Oh, I still have it, but it's not the same any more. It's a separate thing existing in me, but no longer truly a part of me. It's in various cavities and tracts, all connected up by threads, living in me like a rat in a system of burrows. Or better, like a hermit crab in a pirated shell. But you know what happens when a hermit crab outgrows its shell? It moves out, finds itself a bigger home. So…this thing in me has tried to vacate—has experimented with the idea, anyway…."

He shuddered, his whole body trembling like jelly.

"Experimented?" It was all I could find to say.

He gulped, nodded, controlled himself. And he sank what was left of his drink before going on. "In the night, a couple of nights ago, it started to eject—from both ends at once—from just about everywhere. Anus, throat, nostrils, you name it. I almost choked to death before they got to me. But by then it had already given up, retreated, *retracted* itself. And I could breathe again. It was like it…like it hadn't wanted to kill me."

I was numb, dumb, couldn't say anything. The way Smiler told it, it was almost as if he'd credited his cancer with intelligence! But then a white movement caught my eye, and I saw with some relief that it was the boys from the ambulance coming for him. He saw them, too, and clutched my arm. And suddenly fear had made his eyes round in his round face. "Peter…." he said. "Peter…."

"It's OK," I grabbed his fist grabbing me. "It's all right. They have to know what they're doing. You said it yourself, remember? You're not going to die."

"I know, I know," he said. "But will it be worth living?"

And then they came and took him to the ambulance. And for a long time I wondered about that last thing he'd said. But of course in the end it turned out he was right….

The car door slammed and the telephone rang at one and the same time, causing me to start. I looked out through the control shack's dusty window and saw Big "C" receding from the car. Apparently everything was OK. And when the telephone rang again I picked it up.

"OK, Peter," Smiler's voice seemed likewise relieved, "you can come on in now."

But as well as relieved I was also afraid. Now of all times—when it was inevitable—I was afraid. Afraid for the future the world might never have if I didn't go in, and for the future I certainly wouldn't have if I did. Until at last common sense prevailed: what the heck, I had no future anyway!

"Something wrong, old friend?" Smiler's voice was soft. "Hey, don't let it get to you. It will be just like the last time you visited me, remember?" His words were careful, innocent yet contrived. And they held a code.

I said "Sure," put the phone down, left the shack and went to the car. If he was ready for it then so was I. It was ominous out there, in Big "C"'s gloom; getting into the car was like entering the vacant lair of some weird, alien animal. The thing was no longer there, but I knew it had been there. It didn't smell, but I could smell and taste it anyway. You would think so, the way I avoided breathing.

And so my throat was dry and my chest was tight as I turned the lights on to drive. To drive through Big "C," to the core which was Ben 'Smiler' Williams. And driving I thought:

I'm traveling down a hollow tentacle, proceeding along a pseudopod, venturing in an alien vein. And it can put a stop to me, kill me any time it wants to. By suffocation, strangulation, or simply by laying itself down on me and crushing me. But it won't because it needs Smiler, needs to appease him, and he has asked to see me.

As he'd said on the telephone, "Just like the last time." Except we both knew it wouldn't be like the last time. Not at all....

The last time:

That had been fifteen months ago when we'd agreed on the boundaries. But to continue at that point would be to leave out what happened in between. And I needed to fill it in, if only to fix my mind on something and so occupy my time for the rest of the journey. It isn't good for your nerves, to drive down a midmorning road in near darkness, through a tunnel of living, frothing, cancerous flesh.

A month after I'd seen Smiler on the beach, Big "C" broke out. Except that's not exactly how it was. I mean, it wasn't how you'd expect. What happened was this:

Back in 2002 when we went through a sticky patch with the USSR and there were several (as yet *still* unsolved) sabotage attempts on some of our missile and space research sites, a number of mobile ICBM and MIRV networks were quickly commissioned and established across the entire USA. Most of these had been quietly decommissioned or mothballed only a year or two later, but not the one covering the Okeechobee region of Florida. That one still existed, with its principal base or railhead at La Belle and arms reaching out as far as Fort Myers in the west, Fort Drum north of the Lake, and Canal Point right on the Lake's eastern shore. Though still maintained in operational order as a deterrent, the rail network now carried ninety per cent of hardware for the Space Center while its military functions were kept strictly low profile. Or they had been, until that night in late August 2024.

Smiler had a night nurse, but the first thing Big "C" did when he emerged was to kill him. That's what we later figured, anyway. The second thing that he did was derail a MIRV bogie on its way through Lakeport. I can't supply details; I only know he did it.

Normally this wouldn't matter much: seventy-five percent of the runs were dummies anyway. But this one was the real thing, one of the two or three times a year when the warheads were in position. And it looked like something had got broken in the derailment, because all of the alarms were going off at once!

The place was evacuated. Lakeport, Venus, Clewiston—all the towns around Lake Okeechobee—the whole shoot. Even the Okeechobee Space Center itself, though not in its entirety; a skeleton crew stayed on there; likewise at the La Belle silos. A decon team was made ready to go in and tidy things up...except that didn't happen. For through all of this activity, Smiler (or rather, Big "C") had somehow contrived to be forgotten and left behind. And what *did* happen was that Smiler got on the telephone to Okeechobee and told them to hold off. No one was to move. Nothing was to happen.

"You'd better listen and listen good," he'd said. "Big 'C' has six MIRVs, each one with eight bombs aboard. And he's got five of them lined up on Washington, London, Tokyo, Berlin and Moscow, though not necessarily in that order. That's forty nukes for five of the world's greatest capitals and major cities within radii of two hundred miles. That's a holocaust, a nuclear winter, the New Dark Age. As for the sixth MIRV: that one's airborne right now! But it won't hurt because he hasn't programmed detonation instructions. It's just a sign to let you all know that he's not kidding and can do what he says he can do."

The MIRV split up north of Jacksonville; bombs came down harmlessly in the sea off Wilmington, Cape Fear, Georgetown, Charleston, Savannah, Jacksonville, Cape Canaveral and Palm Beach. After that...while no one was quite sure just exactly who Big 'C' was, certainly they all knew he had them by the short and curlies.

Of course, that was when the "news" broke about Smiler's cancer, the fact that it was different. And the cancer experts from the Lakeport Center, and the space medics, too, arrived at the same conclusion: that somehow alien "radiations" or emanations had changed Smiler's cancer into Big "C." The Lakeport doctors and scientists had intended that when it vacated Smiler they'd kill it, but now Big "C" was threatening to kill us, indeed the world. It was then that I remembered how Smiler had credited the thing with intelligence, and now it appeared he'd been right.

So...maybe the problem could have been cleared up right there and then. But at what cost? Big "C" had demonstrated that he knew his way around our weaponry, so if he was going to die why not take us with him? Nevertheless, it's a fact that there were some itchy fingers among the military brass right about that time.

Naturally, we had to let Moscow, London and all the other target areas in on it, and their reaction was about what was expected:

"For God's sake—placate the thing! Do as it tells you—*whatever* it tells you!" And the Sovs said: "If you let anything come out of Florida heading for Moscow, comrades, that's war!"

And then, of course, there was Smiler himself. Big "C" had Smiler in there—a hero, and one of the greatest of all time. So the hotheads cooled down pretty quickly, and for some little time there was a lot of hard, cold, calculated thinking going on as the odds were weighed. But always it came out in Big "C"'s favor. Oh, Smiler and his offspring were only a small percentage of life on Earth, right enough, and we could stand their loss…but what if we attacked and this monstrous growth actually *did* press the button before we nailed him? Could he, for instance, monitor incoming hardware from space? No, for he was at Lakeport and the radar and satellite monitoring equipment was at La Belle. So maybe we could get him in a preemptive strike! A lot of fingernails were chewed. But:

Smiler's next message came out of La Belle, before anybody could make any silly decisions. "Forget it," he warned us. "He's several jumps ahead of you. He made me drive him down here, to La Belle. And this is the deal: *Big 'C' doesn't want to harm anyone*—but neither does he want to be harmed. Here at La Belle he's got the whole world laid out on his screens—*his* screens, have you got that? The La Belle ground staff—that brave handful of guys who stayed on—they're…finished. They opposed him. So don't go making the same mistake. All of this is Big "C"'s now. He's watching everything from space, on radar…all the skills we had in those areas are now his. And he's nervous because he knows we kill things that frighten us, and he supposes that he frightens us. So the minute our defense satellites stop cooperating—the very *minute* he stops receiving information from his radar or pictures from space—he presses the button. And you'd better believe there's stuff here at La Belle that makes that derailed junk at Lakeport look like Chinese firecrackers!" And of course we knew there was.

So that was it: stalemate, a Mexican standoff. And there were even groups who got together and declared that Big "C" had a right to live. If the Israelis had been given Israel, (they argued) the Palestinians Beirut and the Aborigines Alice Springs all the way out to Simpson Desert, then why shouldn't Big "C" have Lake Okeechobee? After all, he was a sentient being, wasn't he? And all he wanted was to live—wasn't it?

Well, that was something of what he wanted, anyway. Moisture from the lake, and air to breathe. And Smiler, of course.

And territory. A lot more territory.

Big "C" grew fast. Very fast. The word "big" itself took on soaring new dimensions. In a few years Big "C" was into all the lakeside towns and spreading outwards. He seemed to live on anything, ate everything, and thrived on it. And it was about then that we decided we really ought to negotiate boundaries. Except "negotiate" isn't the right word.

Smiler asked to see me; I went in; through Smiler Big "C" told me what he wanted by way of land. And he got it. You don't argue with something that can reduce your planet to radioactive ashes. And now that Big "C" was into all the towns and villages on the Lake, he'd moved his nukes in with him. He hadn't liked the idea of having all his eggs in one basket, as it were.

But between Big "C"'s emergence from Smiler and my negotiating the boundaries, Christ knows we tried to get him! Frogmen had gone up the Miami, Hillsboro, and St Lucie canals to poison the Lake—and hadn't come down again. A manmade anthrax variant had been sown in the fields and swamps where he was calculated to be spreading—and he'd just spread right on over it. A fire had started "accidentally" in the long hot summer of 2019, in the dried-out Okaloacoochee Slough, and warmed Big "C"'s hide all the way to the Lake before it died down. But that had been something he couldn't ignore.

"You must be crazy!" Smiler told us that time. "He's launched an ICBM to teach you a lesson. At ten megs its the smallest thing he's got—but still big enough!"

It was big enough for Hawaii, anyway. And so for a while we'd stopped trying to kill him, but we never stopped thinking about it. And someone thought:

If Big "C"'s brain is where Smiler is, and if we can get to that brain…will that stop the whole thing dead?

It was a nice thought. We needed somebody on the inside, but all we had was Smiler. Which brings me back to that time fifteen months ago when I went in to negotiate the new boundaries.

At that time Big "C" was out as far as ten miles from the Lake and expanding rapidly on all fronts. A big round nodule of him extended to cover La Belle, tapering to a tentacle reaching as far as Alva. I'd entered him at Alva as per instructions, where Big "C" had checked the car, then driven on through La Belle on my way to Lakeport, which was now his HQ. And then, as now, I'd passed through the landscape, which he opened for me, driving through his ever-expanding tissues. But I won't go into that here, nor into my conversation with Smiler. Let it suffice to say that Smiler intimated he would like to die now and it couldn't come quickly enough, and that before I left I'd passed him a note which read:

> Smiler,
> The next time someone comes in here he'll be a volunteer, and he'll be bringing something with him. A little something for Big "C." But it's up to you when that happens, good buddy. You're the only one who can fix it.
> Peter

And then I was out of there. But as he'd glanced at the note there had been a look on Smiler's face that was hard to gauge. He'd *told* me that Big "C" only used him as a mouthpiece and as his…host. That the hideous stuff could only instruct him, not read his mind or get into his brain. But as I went to my car that time I could feel Big "C" gathering himself—like a big cat bunching its muscles—and as I actually got into the car something wet, a spot of slime, splashed down on me from overhead! Jesus! It was like the bastard was drooling on me!

"Jesus," yes. Because when I'd passed Smiler that note and he'd looked at me, and we'd come to our unspoken agreement, I hadn't known that *I* would be the volunteer! But I was, and for two reasons: my life didn't matter any more, and Smiler had asked for me—if I was willing. Now that was a funny thing in itself because it meant that he was asking me to die with him. But the thought didn't dawn on me that maybe he knew something that he shouldn't know. Nor would it dawn on me until I only had one more mile to go to my destination, Lakeport. When in any case there was no way I could turn back.

As for what that something was: it was the fact that I too was now dying of cancer.

It was diagnosed just a few weeks after I'd been to see him: the fast-moving sort that was spreading through me like a fire. Which was why I said: sure, I'll come in and see you, Smiler…

Ostensibly I was going in to negotiate the boundaries again. Big "C" had already crossed the old lines and was now out from the lake about forty miles in all directions, taking him to the Atlantic coast in the east and very nearly the Gulf of Mexico in the west. Immokalee had been my starting point, just a mile southwest of where he sprawled over the Slough, and now I was up as far as Palmdale and turning right for Moore Haven and Lakeport. And up to date with my morbid memories, too.

From Palmdale to Lakeport is about twenty-five miles. I drove that narrow strip of road with flaps and hummocks of leprous dough crawling, heaving and tossing on both sides—or clearing from the tarmac before my spinning wheels—while an opaque webbing of alien flesh pulsed and vibrated overhead. It was like driving down the funnel-trap of some cosmic trapdoor spider, or crossing the dry bed of an ocean magically cleared as by Moses and his staff. Except that *this* sea—this ocean of slime and disease—was its own master and cleared the way itself.

And in my jacket pocket my cigarette lighter, and under its hinged cap the button. And I was dying for a cigarette but couldn't have one, not just yet. But (or so I kept telling myself, however ridiculously) that was a good thing because they were bad for you!

The bomb was in the hollow front axle of the car, its two halves sitting near the wheels along with the propellant charges. When those charges detonated they'd drive two loads of hell into calamitous collision right there in the middle of the axle, creating critical mass and instant oblivion for anything in the immediate vicinity. I was driving a very special car: a kamikaze nuke. And ground zero was going to be Big "C"'s brain and my old pal Smiler. And myself, of course.

The miles were passing very quickly now, seeming to speed up right along with my heartbeat, I guessed I could do it even before I got there if I wanted to, blow the bastard to hell. But I wasn't going to give him even a split second's warning, because it was possible that was all he needed. No, I was going to park this heap right up his nose. Almost total disintegration for a radius of three or four miles when it went. For me, for Smiler, but especially for Big "C." Instantaneous, so that he wouldn't even have time to twitch.

And with this picture in mind I was through Moore Haven and Lakeport was up ahead, and I thought: *We've got him! Just two or three more miles and I can let 'er rip any time! And it's goodbye Big "C."* But I wouldn't do it because I wanted to see Smiler one last time. It was him and me together. I could smile right back at him (would I be able to? God, I hoped so!) as I pressed the button.

And it was then, with only a mile to go to Lakeport, that I remembered what Smiler had said the last time he asked for a visitor. He'd said: Someone should come and see me soon, to talk about boundaries *if for nothing else.* I think maybe Peter Lancing…if he's willing."

The "if for nothing else" was his way of saying: "OK, bring it on in." And the rest of it….

The way I saw it, it could be read two ways. That "if he's willing" bit could be a warning, meaning: "Of course, this is really a job for a volunteer." Or he could simply have been saying good-bye to me, by mentioning my name in his final communication. But…maybe it could be read a third way, too. Except that would mean that he *knew* I had cancer, and that therefore I probably would be willing.

And I remembered that blob of goo, that *sweat* or *spittle* of Big "C," which had splashed on me when I was last in here….

Thought processes, and while they were taking place the mile was covered and I was in. It had been made simple: Big "C" had left only one road open, the one that led to the grounds of the Cancer Research Foundation. Some irony, that this should be Big "C"'s HQ! But yes, just looking at the place I knew that it was.

It was…*wet*-looking, glistening, alive. Weakened light filtered down through the layers of fretted, fretting webs of mucus and froth and foaming flesh overhead, and the Foundation complex itself looked like a gigantic, suppurating mass of decaying brick and concrete. Tentacles of filth had shattered all the windows outwards, for all the world as if the building's brain had burst out through its eyes, ears and nostrils. And the whole thing was connected by writhing ropes of webbing to the far greater mass which was Big "C"'s loathsome body.

Jesus! It was gray and green and brown and blue-tinged. In spots it was even bright yellow, red, and splashed with purple. It was Cancer with a capital C—Big "C" himself—and it was alive!

"What are you waiting for, Peter?" Smiler's voice came out of my radio, and I banged my head on the car roof starting away from it. "Are you coming in, old friend…or what?"

I didn't have to go in there if I didn't want to; my lighter was in my pocket; I touched it to make sure. But…I didn't want to go out alone. I don't just mean out like out of the car, but out period. And so:

"I'm coming in, Smiler," I told him.

And somehow I made myself. In front of the main building there'd been lawn cropped close as a crewcut. Now it was just soil crumbling to sand. I walked across it and into the building, just looking straight ahead and nowhere else. Inside…the corridors were clear at least. Big "C" had cleared them for me. But through each door as I passed them I could see him bulking, pile upon pile of him like…like heaped intestines. His brains? God, I hoped so!

Finally, when I was beginning to believe I couldn't go any further on two feet and would have to crawl—and when I was fighting with myself not to throw up—I found Smiler in his "office": just a large room with a desk which he sat behind, and a couple of chairs, telephones, radios. And also containing Big "C," of course. Which is the part I've always been reluctant to talk about, but now have to tell just the way it was.

Big "C" was plugged into him, into Smiler. It was grotesque. Smiler sat propped up in his huge chair, and he was like a spider at the center of his web. Except the web wasn't of silk but of flesh, and it was attached to him. The back of his head was welded to a huge fan-shape of tentacles spreading outwards like some vast ornamental headdress, or like the sprawl of an octopus's arms; and these cancerous extensions or extrusions were themselves attached to a shuddering bulk that lay behind Smiler's chair and grew up the walls and out of the windows. The lower part of his body was lost behind the desk, lost in bulging grey sacks and folds and yellow pipes and purplish gelatinous masses of...Christ, of whatever the filthy stuff was! Only his upper body, his arms and hands, face and shoulders were free of the stuff. He was it. It was him—physically, anyway.

No one could have looked at him and felt anything except disgust, or perhaps pity if they'd known him like I had. And if they hadn't, dread and loathing and...yes, horror. Friendship didn't come into it; I knew that I wasn't smiling; I knew that my face must reflect everything I felt.

He nodded the merest twitch of a nod and husked: "Sit down, Peter, before you fall down! Hey, and you think I look bad, right?" Humor! Unbelievable! But his voice was a desiccated whisper, and his grey hands on the desk shook like spindly skating insects resting up after a morning's hard skimming over a stagnant pond.

I sat down on a dusty chair opposite him, perching myself there, feeling all tight inside from not wanting to breathe the atmosphere, and hypersensitive outside from trying not to touch anything. He noticed and said: "You don't want to contaminate yourself, right? But isn't it a bit late for that, Peter?"

From which I could tell that he knew—he *did* know—and a tingle started in my feet that quickly surged through my entire being. Could he see it in me? Sense it in me? Feel some sort of weird kinship with what was under my skin, burgeoning in me? Or was it worse than that? And right there and then I began to have this feeling that things weren't going according to plan.

"Smiler," I managed to get started at the second attempt, "it's...*good* to see you again, pal. And I...." And I stopped and just sat there gasping.

"Yes?" he prompted me in a moment. "And you—?"

"Nerves!' I gasped, forcing a sickly smile, and forced in my turn to take my first deep breath. "Lots of nerves. It was always the same. It's why I had to stay behind when you and the others went into space." And I took out my cigarettes, and also took out the lighter from my pocket. I opened the pack and shook out several cigarettes, which fell on the floor, then managed to trap one between my knees and transfer it shakily to my mouth. And I flipped back the top on my lighter.

Smiler's eyes—the only genuinely mobile parts he had left—went straight to the lighter and he said: "You brought it in, right?" But should he be saying things like that? Out loud, I mean? Couldn't Big "C" hear him or sense his mood? And it dawned on me just how little we knew about them, about Big "C" and Smiler—as he was now….

Then…Smiler smiled. Except it wasn't his smile!

Goodbye, everything, I said to myself, pressing the button and holding my thumb down on it. Then releasing it and pressing it again, and again. And finally letting the fucking thing fall from my nerveless fingers when, after two or three more tries, *still* nothing had happened. Or rather, "nothing" hadn't happened.

"Peter, old buddy, let me tell you how it is." Smiler got through to me at last, as the cigarette fell from my trembling lips. "I mean, I suspect you now *know* how it is, but I'll tell you anyway. See, Big 'C' changes things. Just about anything he wants to change. He was nothing at first, or not very much—just a natural law of change, mutation, entropy if you like. An 'emanation.' Or on the other hand I suppose you could say he was everything—like Nature itself. Whichever, when I went up there to Luna II he got into me and changed my cancer into himself, since when he's become one hell of a lot. We can talk about that in a minute, but first I want to explain about your bomb. Big 'C' changed it. He changed the chemical elements of the explosive charges, and to be doubly sure sucked all the fizz out of the fissionable stuff. It was a firework and he dumped it in a bucket of water. So now you can relax. It didn't go off and it isn't going to."

"You…*are* him!" I knew it instinctively. Now, when it was too late. "But when? And why?"

"When did I stop being Smiler? Not long after that time you met him at the beach. And why the subterfuge? Because you human beings are a jumpy lot. With Smiler to keep you calm, let you think you had an intermediary, it was less likely you'd do something silly. And why should I care that you'd do something silly? Because there's a lot of life, knowledge, sustenance in this Earth and I didn't want you killing it off trying to kill me! But now you can't kill me, because the bigger I've got the easier it has become to change things. Missiles? Go ahead and try it. They'll be dead before they hit me. Why, if I got the idea you were going to try firing a couple, I could even kill them on the ground!

"You see, Peter, I've grown too big, too clever, too devious to be afraid any more—of anything. Which is why I have no more secrets, and why there'll be no more subterfuge. Subterfuge? Not a bit of it. Why, I'm even broadcasting all of this—just so the whole world will know what's going on! I mean, I *want* them to know, so no one will make any more silly mistakes. Now, I believe you came in here to talk about boundaries—some limits you want to see on my expansion?"

Somehow, I shook my head. "That's not why I'm here, Smiler," I told him, not yet ready to accept that there was nothing of Smiler left in there. "Why I'm here is finished now."

"Not quite," he said, but very quietly. "We can get to the boundaries later, but there is something else. Think about it. I mean, why should I want to see you, if there's nothing else and if I can make any further decisions without outside help?"

"I don't know. Why?"

"See, Smiler has lasted a long time. Him and the frogmen that came to kill me, and a couple of farmers who didn't get out fast enough when they saw me coming, oh, and a few others. And I've been instructed by them. Like I said: I've learned how to be devious. And I've learned anger, too, though there's no longer any need for that. No need for any human emotions. But the last time you came to see Smiler—and when you would have plotted with him to kill me—that angered me."

"And so you gave me my cancer."

"Yes I did. So that when I needed you, you'd *want* to be my volunteer. But don't worry…you're not going to die, Peter. Well, not physically anyway, and not just yet a while. For just like Smiler here, you're going to carry on."

"But no anger, eh? No human emotions? No…revenge? OK, so let me go free to live out what days I've got left."

"No anger, no revenge, no emotions—just need. I *can't* let you go! But let me explain myself. Do you know what happens when you find a potato sprouting in your vegetable rack and you plant it in the garden? That's right, you get lots of new potatoes! Well, I'm something like that. I'm putting out lots of new potatoes, lots of new me. All of the time. And the thing is this: when you dig up those potatoes and your fork goes through the old one, what do you find? Just a wrinkled, pulpy old sack of a thing all ready to collapse in upon itself, with nothing of goodness left in it—pretty much like what's left of Smiler here. So…if I want to keep growing potatoes, why,

I just have to keep planting them! Do you see?"

"Jesus! *Jesus!*"

"It's nothing personal, Peter. It's need, that's all…No, don't stand up, just sit there and I'll do the rest. And you can stop biting down on that clever tooth of yours, because it isn't poison any more, just salt. And if you don't like what's happening to Smiler right now, that's OK—just turn your face away…

"…There, that was pretty easy, now wasn't it?

"All you people out there, that's how it is. So get used to it. As for the new boundaries: there aren't any.

This is Big "C," signing off."